DISTANT THUNDER

Gods & Thunder – Book One

Lilli Carlisle

ALSO BY LILLI CARLISLE

FATED MATES

Tigress

Huntress

Speechless

Merciless

THE BLACK RIDGE WOLF PACK

Omega's Choice

Ceva's Chance

Karli's Resolve

Laura's Legacy

Lili's Trust

Katrina's Destiny

www.BOROUGHSPUBLISHINGGROUP.com

PUBLISHER'S NOTE: This is a work of fiction. Names, characters, places and incidents either are the product of the author's imagination or are used fictitiously. Any resemblance to actual events, locales, business establishments or persons, living or dead, is coincidental. Boroughs Publishing Group does not have any control over and does not assume responsibility for author or third-party websites, blogs or critiques or their content.

DISTANT THUNDER
Copyright © 2020 LILLI CARLISLE

ISBN 978-1-951055-87-5

This has been possible only with the love and support of my family.
Love you Craig, Samantha, Katie, and Jason.

DISTANT THUNDER

Chapter One

Net stood, admired her handiwork, and smiled. She may not have her powers back yet, but she could plant flowers instead of using her magic to bring them to life. She enjoyed doing this. Getting her hands dirty, connecting with the earth in a way she hadn't felt before when she willed things into existence.

It had been many months since the judgment, and she was still settling into her new home. Net was under house arrest at the shifter god Fenrir's home. He was seldom here, leaving her lonely, yet giving her time for introspection. Without her powers, Net was vulnerable to attack from not only the demon population, who would love nothing better than to pick off a goddess, but the other gods as well.

Some gods were known to be petty, quickly taking offense over any little thing. As was the way with most politics, an individual was never really sure a god was gunning for them until it was too late. Typically, when she had her powers, Net had no fear of her brethren. She shared their strength, immortality, and she had her unique magic. At full power, Net wasn't an easy target. Fortunately, for now, things had been quiet. Fenrir's protection spells held, and no one had tried to attack her.

She would be happy if she made it through her punishment unscathed. She had to admit, she missed her connection to the greater natural world. As the goddess of the forests and the plants, divine mother of nature, she used to be able to feel the ebb and flow of every being big or small, animal or plant. Now, in a world without her powers, things quieted in her mind and body in a way that made her feel she'd lost what made her Net. Yet, at the same time, the narrowness of her existence made her appreciate every little thing.

She scanned the front yard of her new home, and prison of sorts, pleased that the rows of flower beds overflowed with blooms of every color and size. Net wasn't sure what she'd do with herself once she'd completed the planting. Perhaps she should plant a few vegetables and add fruit trees to the mix. Even strawberries would serve her well. She loved the sweet fruit.

It wasn't as though Fenrir's home was a hovel. Quite the opposite. The large cottage was set in a glorious forest, keeping her in touch with her core strengths, and giving her lots of space to roam. She picked up her small shovel and watering bucket, deciding that the last flower bed had been enough for today. She stowed the implements in the little shed and was on her way back to the house when an alarm sounded.

The first of Fenrir's defenses were under attack. *Fates*. Another alarm sounded, and she began running for the safety of the cottage where protection was the strongest. She had barely stepped over the threshold of the front door when the third and last alarm sounded.

She'd tempted fate to have thought about the quiet and calm. She felt somehow she'd sent out a challenge. When would she learn to keep her thoughts to herself?

She bolted the door, sealing the last spell in place. Fenrir was going to be angry someone messed with his home. The inside of the cottage held an iridescence, which covered the exterior walls, doors, and windows, a visual confirmation the protection spell was in place and holding.

"Sister. Won't you come out to play?" a familiar voice yelled from the front yard.

It couldn't be.

Net went to the window to make sure she wasn't losing her mind and gasped as Vengier waved at her from his perch in the center of one of her new flower beds. He stood in what was left of her plants. So like him to destroy every beautiful thing in his path. The former god of beauty was too vindictive to allow anything that held promise, hope, or abundance exist around him.

Taking a closer look, she had to say Vengier wasn't looking himself, unless he was going for the zombie version of the god of beauty. Perhaps it was his vile nature finally showing through, much like the human story *The Portrait of Dorian Gray*, with one not-so-small difference: Vengier was dead.

The rings of gold on her wrists warmed, letting her know the cavalry was on the way. "Tell me, brother, who put the pieces of you back together? Whoever's magic was used they didn't do even a mediocre job. You look awful."

"I have friends much stronger than you can even imagine," he boasted, as if gaping holes in his body and the odd piece falling to the ground were something to rejoice about.

"Couldn't be too strong if they left you looking like roadkill." Seriously, parts of his face looked ready to slide off.

The cottage shook as Vengier lobbed counter-spells, attempting to break through the last barrier. "You think cursing you to remain in that forest after I took care of that little mate problem of yours was painful? Oh, sister, you have not begun to feel pain."

How Vengier ended up such a vile and hateful creature was a case study in narcissism. After Fenrir had raked his claws down one side of Vengier's face in retaliation for killing Fenrir's mate centuries ago, Vengier had lost his sanity. Leaving the once-conceited god scarred for life was perhaps the worst thing anyone could have done to him. He valued his appearance above all else, and marred, he became a hateful, evil thing.

"Have you not caused me enough damage?" Net asked. As if killing her mate and cursing her to an eternity locked inside a forest as her precious flora died around her wasn't enough, he'd forced her to watch as her mate was reborn and grew among a nearby pack without so much as a scintilla of memory of her, them, and what they'd shared.

"It won't be enough until you're dead," Vengier raged. "I'll leave you gutted for Fenrir to find, exactly as I did with his mate."

"I don't know how many times we need to kill you to make it final, but we'll enjoy trying until it sticks. Don't worry, this time I'll spread your ashes so far apart no one will be able to bring you back," Net shouted, trying to buy time for Fenrir to arrive. What was taking him so long?

As if reading her mind. "If you're waiting for the mutt to come to save you, I'm sorry to tell you his wolf-ness won't be joining us this evening," Vengier said. Net wanted to summon her dormant power and zap him a good one to knock that smirk off his face. "I sent a few of my new friends to keep him busy. I wouldn't want him to ruin our alone time, sis."

"Suddenly, you have a whole slew of friends. I find it odd considering most of the gods despise you." That left only demons.

Net knew by taunting him she was adding wood to her own pyre, but she couldn't engage him without her powers, and she wasn't going to go down without some sort of fight.

"No worries, sister mine. Everyone will know of my friends soon enough. Then, we'll enjoy ridding ourselves of those who think we need to follow archaic rules and codes. We're gods. We make the rules. I'm almost sorry you won't be around to see what happens to your favored shifters when we take over."

"Take over. Seriously, who has been filling that decomposing brain with that fantasy?" she asked while forcing a laugh. "Or did they forget to stitch it back into your skull altogether?"

Her bracelets were still warm, so that meant Fenrir was close.

"Enough talk, sister." Vengier's voice boomed through the cottage. She must have hit a nerve. "It is time for you to die."

The air crackled with energy, and the cottage shook again. A few pots fell from their hooks, a clanging and smashing ruckus when they hit the floor. Net was starting to have second thoughts about the wisdom of poking at her crazy-ass brother.

Another jarring strike had the table sliding to the other side of the kitchen. She braced herself against a wall as the world trembled around her. Precious pottery that had no doubt belonged to Fenrir's deceased mate fell like rain from the open shelves. Net's heart ached at the destruction of such a cherished memory, and seeing it increased her anger tenfold.

Explosions hammered against the last barrier still standing between them when suddenly her bracelets went ice cold. No, that couldn't be right. Net experienced a moment of genuine fear until she heard the deep voice of the god who would save her.

"Vengier, shouldn't you be in a plot somewhere?" Fenrir growled, his voice booming above the magical explosions.

Net uncurled her body and stood to look out the newly cracked window. Sure enough, Fenrir, in his black wolf form, stood between her demented brother and the cottage. Fenrir's voice rang through the air as with all gods. There was no need for him to be in his human form to communicate out loud.

She couldn't remember ever seeing him in his human form. Impressive as he might be as a wolf, she had a feeling he was even better as a man.

Knowing how fierce he was about the beings under his protection, Net waited for the fun to begin.

***

Fenrir stood as wolf in front of his cottage. There was no way he'd allow Vengier pass. In truth, he was angry the bastard made it this far.

"Well, hello, wolfie. Come to try to save another woman from certain death in your home?" Vengier taunted, crossing his almost skeletal arms across his puzzle-piece chest.

Vengier had killed Fenrir's mate centuries ago. She had been a wolf shifter, part of a pack, and this bastard had attacked her when Fenrir was away. However, he'd learned long ago to show no weakness, and pretended the nasty reminder didn't affect him. Fenrir wouldn't dishonor his beloved's memory by engaging this craven bastard in any discussion involving Fenrir's deceased mate.

"You remain pathetic, Vengier. Now at least your stench matches your appearance. I recommend you tie an air freshener around your neck, or soap on a rope. Something." The smell of decomposition was ripe in the air. "Here's a wild thought, how about wearing a few of those flowers instead of standing on them."

Vengier growled and lobbed a fireball toward the cottage roof. It hit one of Fenrir's barrier spells, and fell to the ground completely extinguished without leaving a single singe mark.

"Seriously, that's all you've got?" Fenrir laughed. "A fledgling could produce more power than that. Perhaps you should leave before I fry what's left of you."

"Don't worry about my power, dog. I grow stronger every day," Vengier boasted. "If I hadn't wasted energy on my 'loving' sister, I'd have you on the ground, writhing in pain by now. The time is soon coming for high and mighty to be a memory."

"Unfortunately for you, today is not that day." Fenrir commanded multiple bolts of lightning to strike down from the blue sky, but the crafty bastard vanished before they hit their mark. Vengier's psychotic laughter floating on the breeze was all that remained of his loathsome presence.

Now that the bastard was gone, Fenrir needed to find out how Vengier made it so close to the cottage, and who was helping him.

The why of it didn't escape Fenrir. Whoever helped "repair" Vengier was using the wastrel as a shill. A disposable commodity in a first assault against the gods. Unfortunately, finding the "whoever" wouldn't take long. Evil couldn't wait to show itself. Vainglorious in its efforts, it danced into view as soon as it could.

Fenrir heard the front door open and turned to find a visibly shaken Net standing on the front stoop. Quickly, he went to her.

"I'm sorry about your home," she said immediately. "I'll clean up and repair the damage."

"Forget about that. Are you hurt?" He could smell blood, and considering she was no longer a goddess, bleeding held a different meaning. Blood loss for mortals was often fatal. He towered over her, even as wolf, the form in which he'd remained since his mate's death centuries before.

She checked herself over before holding up her right arm, revealing a gash on the back of her forearm. "Huh, I wonder why I didn't feel any pain?"

"You were scared for your life. Your body was in fight-or-flight mode, thinking of ways to save itself." Adrenaline was a powerful drug. In battle, he'd seen others continue to fight even after a grave injury.

"True enough. Even though it was only my vile half-decomposed brother, he still managed to shake me up." She dabbed the bleeding wound with the hem of her dress. "Until recently, I've not yet fully understood how fragile the mortal body is."

"Let me see your arm," he ordered.

When she lifted her arm to him, he licked over the gash and watched as the flesh knitted together. He always found human blood to be metallic in taste, not something he enjoyed, which was odd for a wolf god.

"It tingles," she remarked, as she too looked transfixed by the wound closing. "Thank you."

Her expression turned sad as she surveyed her flower gardens. From the shadows of the forest surrounding the cottage, he'd watched her work on them for weeks. Now the colorful blooms and thick vines were mulched into a mess of dirt, roots, and broken petals.

"I can fix your flowers," Fenrir offered and was about to revive them when she laid her small hand on the thick fur around his neck.

"No. It's fine," she said. "I'll start over. Replanting will help occupy my time."

He understood. She'd had her powers taken away as punishment for attempting to have a wolf shifter killed. She'd been placed in a situation where events unfolded around her that were beyond her control, and her actions were made in haste.

Her brother was responsible for her mate's death, killing her beloved because he'd been a wolf shifter, not a god. She'd spent centuries trapped in that same forest as the earth slowly died around her, cut off from contact with mortals and other gods. Her reaction to a perceived hostile situation was understandable, but regrettable.

When she was failing, and the altercation was becoming intense, he'd responded to her call for help. His answer had been to allow Bain, her former mate, to be reborn. The only conditions were that Bain would never remember her or the love they'd shared, and, due to the physical damage to his legs, he'd never walk again.

Net was being held unfairly accountable for others' actions. This was why, until she got her powers back, he intended to keep her safe in his home.

"If that is what you wish."

He knew she was lonely here with him being away a good portion of the time dealing with other gods, and watching over his shifters. She was right. Re-creating the beautiful gardens would help her pass the time.

"Yes, it is. Thank you for the kind offer," she said while shaking her head at the ruins of her hard work. "Are you hungry? Do you have time for a visit?"

Her eyes seemed to sparkle with hope, and there was no way he'd disappoint her. "Yes, that sounds lovely." Fenrir had been absent and was now beginning to regret his decision to keep himself hidden away from her so she could heal from all her losses.

Her smile had always held the power to turn him into mush, but no one ever need know the truth of that. If others knew, she'd have an even bigger target on her back. He'd already been the cause of his mate's death. He refused to add another.

He followed her into his cottage, watching as she picked broken bits up as they went. Pots, cups, a vase of flowers all lay scattered across the floor. If those demons hadn't attacked the pack in Black Ridge, one of the many wolf shifter packs he watched over in another realm, he would have been here sooner. Sadly, the old pieces of pottery he'd kept as mementos from his mate lay shattered on the floor.

He felt waves of regret and grief coming from Net as she surveyed the damage. "I'm sorry about the pottery. If there was a way to make them whole once again, I would gladly do it."

Earlier, while locked in battle, Fenrir had felt her fear and anger through the golden rings he'd given her to wear around her wrists. Knowing the protective barriers he'd created would slow whoever was near his cottage allowed him to vanquish the demons and make it back home in time.

"I could return everything to the way it was before Vengier's visit," Fenrir offered as she reached for the pieces of a clay bowl she'd painted to resemble a daisy.

"If you wish to do so with the pottery, please do, but nothing else on my behalf," she answered in a calm voice. "I'm trying to embrace the powerless mortal position I find myself in. Who knows, this might be irreversible."

He nodded, and with a thought and the blink of an eye, the cottage went from disarray back to everything in its place.

She turned and surveyed the space, sighing. He felt her pain waft off her body. She could've done that herself if her powers hadn't been stripped. He wanted to reassure her, even though most of what he said was conjecture and wishful thinking.

"It's not permanent," he stated. "I guarantee it."

"Did The Judge, Forseti, say that?" Her expression was hopeful.

Forseti was a god known as The Judge. He held power to punish other gods and goddesses for misdeeds, and for breaking the rules and laws that governed them.

"Yes, though he didn't see fit to tell me when that would be." A timeline would have been helpful.

Net shrugged and carried on into the kitchen. Fenrir noticed the subtle changes in his home as they went. There was a warmth now inside what used to be cold walls. He hadn't spent much time here over the last three centuries, mainly since his mate had died. Now, the place felt lit with life and color once again.

The smell of fresh bread filled the air as well as vegetable stew bubbling on the stove. Of course, he'd made sure the cupboards were always filled for her, now that she required food regularly. Gods enjoyed food and cooking, but it wasn't necessary to sustain them. One of the realities of their immortality.

"Have the cupboards been cooperating with your wishes?" Fenrir asked. He had enchanted them so that they gave Net whatever she needed, from food to eat and seeds to plant, to clothes to wear and items needed around the cottage.

"Yes, they've been helpful. Anything I ask they produce," Net said while looking down at her bloody clothing. "I'm going to go clean up before dinner. I shouldn't be long."

Fenrir nodded before padding into his living room to find even more of her touches. Throw pillows and blankets covered both chairs and the couch, and new drapes in a vibrant array of colors replaced the old faded ones, which had hung to the rod by their threads. The fireplace had been cleaned, and new logs were arranged on the metal stand, kindling at the ready. All the windows were clear, and their corners free of cobwebs.

It wasn't that Fenrir was a slob, but he'd been avoiding the cottage and had done the bare minimum to it for a long time. New life filled the rooms, and what had been little more than a shell that held a few precious memories was now a home. He liked the feeling and the emotions that came along with the changes. Would it be so wrong to want Net to be his? He had no idea how she saw him, or if she was even open to the possibility.

"I'm sorry," Net said yet again. The term was becoming a habit he wasn't overly fond of. "I should have asked before I made any changes to your home. You're away most of the time, and I may have gotten carried away." Net glanced around, taking in everything. "Okay, I admit it. I did get carried away."

Fenrir looked down at her. "Stop saying you're sorry. You didn't do anything wrong. I left you with a cottage that hadn't been lived in for centuries. You have every right to make where you live comfortable." He felt like an idiot. Why hadn't he thought about at least cleaning up the place before dropping her off and disappearing? He should've told her she had free rein to do as she pleased upfront.

"This is all strange and new to me. I'm not sure if I'm doing anything right. As a goddess, I never once felt unsure of my actions; there was never a need. Now, I'm mentally exhausted second-guessing myself, and I'm trying to deal with my decisions as best as

I can. Then something happens, and I'm questioning myself over again."

Yeah, he's an idiot. He couldn't imagine what it would feel like to exist without his powers. Vaguely, he'd considered her circumstance and had enchanted the cupboards and cabinets, but processing how lost she must feel, how out of place and disoriented, he never gave it a thought. He left with spells and protections in place and went about his business.

"That brings us to my second point. As far as I'm concerned, treat this place as your home. Do what you will. So far, the place is looking better every time I visit."

Net blushed. Had he ever seen her blush before now? Fenrir doubted it. If she had, he most assuredly would have remembered seeing it. She was stunning, inside and out.

"Thank you, I haven't had a framed home in millennia," she remarked with a contented smile. "I rather enjoy the feel of this one. It's peaceful, warm, and well situated. From the floorboards to the timber beams, I find myself wanting to curl up in that oversize chair in front of the fire every night."

"I swear to you, I'll strengthen the spells and protections, and I'll add more safety barriers around the cottage, especially since we know your brother's back and has made friends with demons. I will not allow you to be harmed again," Fenrir assured. He wouldn't allow her to be caught unprepared a second time. "It means a lot having you here, Net. The place has come alive once again. It's good to see and does this old wolf's heart good."

"Won't Forseti be able to capture Vengier? The Judge had no problem kidnapping me, locking me up, putting me on trial, if you can call it that, and then banishing my powers. Apprehending one decomposing god shouldn't cause any difficulty."

Net and Forseti didn't see eye to eye on more than a few things. Most of their antagonism had been based on his son mating with Net. He blamed Net for Bain's injuries and subsequent loss of memory after being reborn. Even though Bain was living happily with his new mates and had reunited with his father, Forsetti's grudge manifested in her punishment. Anyone else would've gotten a slap on the wrist.

Knowing she was powerless and on her own, Fenrir hadn't wanted to tell her about the bizarre happenings that had been plaguing gods, shifters, witches, and many other creatures throughout different dimensions and worlds, but the time had come.

"A few odd events have occurred over the past year, and we believe the fact that Forseti is missing is a major reason for what has been happening."

Net's eyes got wider, and her mouth fell open. "Forseti is missing? He's the strongest god in existence. What's going on?"

"I didn't want to worry you, especially now," he explained. "Let's eat first, and after, I'll tell you everything I know." Net had made what looked and smelled like a delicious meal, and he didn't want to ruin it. What he had to say would surely accomplish that.

Her jade green eyes look troubled, and he hated that he'd caused that. On the other hand, she was a goddess—albeit powerless for now—she had every right to know what was going on.

"I agree. Let's eat. I'm not going to like what you have to tell me. We'll enjoy our meal together before we delve into your bad news and undoubtedly ruin our evening."

Fenrir dropped his head and followed her into the kitchen.

Net pulled out a plate and bowl from the cupboard and set them on the oak dining table along with a potholder before returning to the stove to retrieve the bubbling pot. Fenrir moved the bread, cutting board and all, with only a thought, placing it beside the pot of stew on the table.

"Thank you," Net said as she laid utensils down beside her plate. Fenrir wouldn't require them.

She moved a kitchen chair out of his way, making room for him at the table, and began to ladle the goodness onto his plate. As he had a moment before, with a mere slip of his power, he cut the bread, placing a piece on Net's bowl and his plate.

The way they moved around each other, the comfort and ease she displayed in creating space for him at the table, her apparent nonchalance at him being in wolf form all the time, it felt as if they'd done this dance for years, though tonight would be the first time they shared a meal since he'd brought her here.

Net hissed when a few drops of gravy splashed up onto her hand when she'd returned the ladle to the pot.

"Are you okay?"

Net smiled even though he could feel her pain radiating from her hand. "Yes, I'm fine. It's a good reminder for me to be more aware of what I'm doing."

"I will heal it for you." Fenrir would never leave her in pain, even a small burn.

Net ran her uninjured hand across the fur on his shoulder. "Thank you, Fenrir. You are truly kind. I'd prefer to leave the burn as it is. It will serve as a reminder for me to be more careful. My distraction didn't cause the previous injury. That was all on Vengier, and I was happy to have you heal it."

Fenrir didn't like the idea of her suffering even for a moment, but he accepted her decision. This was her path to follow, and whatever came next would be up to her. However, if she were in more pain than a tiny skin burn, he'd heal her without question, and he didn't care if she barked at him for doing it.

They ate in companionable silence, well, other than his moans between bites. Net was one hell of a cook if dinner was indicative of her abilities. She served him a full second plate, and Fenrir finished it all. The stew had thick gravy, spices, delicious vegetables cut into cubes, potatoes, and a few vegetables. The bread was crusty on the outside and soft within, just the way he liked it. Dinner had been perfect. He hated that he had to wreck the remainder of their evening talking about what was going on in their world.

Fenrir didn't allow Net to clean up. She'd done the cooking. Within moments he had the dishes cleaned and back in the cupboards. She watched under hooded lids, and again he didn't consider the ramifications of watching him wield his powers when she didn't have hers anymore.

"I suppose we should get down to the bad news," she said before taking a spot on the couch and covering herself with one of the new blankets. "So, tell me, what's been happening beyond my gilded cage?"

Chapter Two

Net curled up on the cushions preparing herself for the worst. Anything could be happening outside of her protective bubble, and she'd be none the wiser. She was cut off from her powers, her people, and the universe. She had never known silence like this.

Fenrir jumped on the sofa beside her before lying down and taking over roughly three-quarters of the couch cushions. The god was huge in his wolf form, and she couldn't help but wonder about his appearance in human form.

"There have been incidents with increasing severity across all realms and species. Forseti has been missing for over three months, and none of the gods have been able to sense him."

"Do you think he was taken, or did he disappear for a reason?"

"The prevailing belief is that he's been forced into seclusion. Our best trackers have been unable to find him in any realm, and a handful of beings have begun to take advantage of his absence."

"I can imagine a few would take advantage, god and demon alike." Net was well aware that some beings barely stayed on the right side of The Judge, and with him gone, there was no one to stop them from acting on their impulses except the other gods.

"Have they been attacking the packs?" Shifters were strong but they were no match for a mob of turncoat gods.

"There have been attacks," Fenrir divulged. "For the time being, we have been able to ward them off."

"We?" It would make sense to create a group in a fight that could potentially change the course of existence.

"Yes. A handful of our kind have joined together, attempting to keep the damage to a minimum until Forseti's return," Fenrir explained. "If he returns."

Net couldn't help but wonder if she knew any of them. Of course, she didn't personally know every god and goddess. It would be akin to one shifter personally knowing all shifters in existence—

an impossibility. Net didn't ask for names, but was grateful Fenrir had help.

"Where could he be? We have always been able to sense The Judge. He made sure of it." He kept the balance in their universe. "Do you think he's dead?"

"I sincerely hope not, or we're in for a war the likes of which have never been seen." He sighed in frustration. "Demons have been making appearances across different lands and worlds."

You could always pick out demons by their soulless, black eyes. You never could tell who they were looking at. Both irises and sclera were dark ebony. Their bodies were a cross between reptile and human. "Were they responsible for my brother being brought back to life so he could make an appearance and threaten us?"

"Yes," Fenrir answered. "They must have some use for him, though I can't imagine what."

"For obvious reasons, there's no love lost between me and Forseti, but I recognize his importance in keeping the balance between gods and demons."

All this upheaval was happening around her while she sat in limbo. She doubted she'd ever felt so helpless and irrelevant. Fenrir held her gaze, and Net shoved her emotions down before he could suspect her self-indulgence. She remained a goddess, even without her powers. If nothing else, her role could be a sounding board for Fenrir, and a tactical guide.

Fenrir jumped off the couch and stood tall in the center of the living room.

"Is something wrong?" Net asked.

"They're calling me back to the same pack attacked earlier," he said while looking at her, his indecision evident.

Net didn't need him hanging around here, watching over her. "Go. You have to go. What if the demons have returned? You have to protect your people."

"You'll be safe here," Fenrir said. "I promise that the perimeter barriers are reinforced, but if you need me, I'll know and come back right away."

She'd always been able to count on Fenrir. "Of course you will. I trust you. Now go."

Fenrir took one last look around the cottage, then his gaze landed on her, and he watched her for a long moment before disappearing.

Net's anger at her inability to help infuriated her. She should be out there protecting the innocent, yet here she sat, in the middle of a forest protected like a coddled child. An impotent and powerless goddess.

Knowing that Forseti might be dead meant she had to deal with the reality that this might be her life for the rest of her years. In mortal form, she had maybe sixty years left, and of those, she might be useful for forty-five. She had to figure out what she could do to help.

She'd learned many useful things as a goddess, and there was nothing wrong with her brain function. If she couldn't wield her powers, she'd provide whatever guidance she could to help her people overcome the evil that threatened them.

***

Fenrir appeared outside the packhouse of the Black Ridge wolves. There was damage everywhere he looked, the same as before he left to help Net.

He padded up the stairs and into the main house even though the door was shut tight. Walls and doors provided no obstacle for gods. They walked straight through the obstructions without leaving a mark.

The living room was crammed with concerned pack members. Aldric, the alpha of the pack, stood at the front along with his beta Godric, and Alpha-Mate Helena. Ceva, a white witch, stood off to the side with the pack's head of security, Lothar.

"Fenrir," Aldric yelled to be heard over the gathered crowd, silencing them immediately. A path appeared in front of him so that he could join the leaders down front. "Is the Goddess Net safe?"

"She is for now." And he was going to damn well keep it that way. "Seems whoever is leading the demon hordes has been busy recruiting. Vengier showed up outside my home."

"Vengier?" Helena asked. "I thought he'd been destroyed."

"I can attest to it," Ceva agreed. "I watched the bastard die in pieces." Vengier was infamous for his hatred of shifters, and there wasn't a single shifter soul who was upset by his demise.

"Well, someone put those pieces back together and sent him to take down Net," Fenrir stated while considering different forms of payback.

"Seems to go hand in hand with the prior ogre attacks and current demon assaults on the packs," Godric said.

"The pattern suggests the same being is directing the attacks. Over the last decade, there has been an uptick in inexplicable occurrences."

First ogres, horrible, nasty creatures, driven by death and destruction, besieged the packs. Recently, the demons had become more aggressive, and their attacks more coordinated. It appeared as if some being had targeted the shifters. Whether the motivation was personal was irrelevant. The leader had to be found and destroyed.

"Other dimensions have experienced bizarre events but not at the same level as here," Fenrir stated.

"I'll increase my protective wards around the pack." Ceva, a powerful white witch, would do as she promised.

"And I will increase my sweeps over the area," Fenrir informed the group. "Until who's behind this is discovered and dealt with, it would be best for the packs to stay on their lands for the time being where it's safest. I don't want to have individual shifters putting themselves at risk."

"Done," Aldric agreed. "I'd prefer my pack close. We are strongest together."

Fenrir nodded before turning and heading toward the backyard where he could see the remaining members of his team. Four gods, fighting to keep the chaos at bay long enough for Forseti to be found.

Meruim, Thiesen, Agomon, and Abba stood waiting for him at the edge of the forest. Meruim appeared rough around the edges. Years spent at war with her father left her irritable and angry most of the time. However, her hatred of demons for killing her sister made her an asset to their cause.

Thiesen had spent most of his existence lounging among other celestial beings without a care in the world. That was up until The Judge vanished and threw their existence into mayhem. Thiesen wanted the universe returned to what it had always been, which allowed him the good fortune of having no responsibilities. His motivation might not be altruistic, but his commitment was unshakeable.

Agomon hailed from a long line of warrior gods. They were often used by The Judge to enforce his rulings and protect the innocent. Agomon had a clear understanding and commitment to the laws governing them, and his ferocity was notorious.

Abba had appeared one day offering his assistance in a battle they fought in another realm. While his help was welcome, Fenrir couldn't say he knew that much about Abba, but he was instrumental in defeating the demons who preyed on this primitive culture.

In that reality, the inhabitants were still in the early stages of their existence, living in caves, hunting with spears, and only beginning to learn how to paint their histories on walls. In those worlds, the gods remained as hands-off as possible to allow the species to develop undisturbed. Then the demons began showing up.

"How is Net?" Agomon asked as Aldric had earlier. It was warming to hear their concern for her until Meruim spoke.

"I'm betting that you found her chopped up into little bits." The bloodthirsty goddess flashed a smile.

Fenrir growled, making Meruim take a couple of steps back. "She is safe, but you would do well to remember how important Net is." He wouldn't take Meruim's shit. She knew it and shrugged in answer.

"Fine." Fenrir wasn't sure where her hatred was coming from and didn't care. She was there to perform a duty that benefitted all of them and the inhabitants of many realms. He shouldn't have to remind her of that.

"It seems as if someone is busy resurrecting old enemies. Vengier has returned," Fenrir stated. "He was pieced back together and was sent to take on his sister."

Thiesen huffed loud and long, in his typically exaggerated fashion. "Did he come back with a new attitude because he was such a downer before?"

Fenrir could hear Meruim's eyes rolling at the pampered god's questions. In truth, a number of gods spent their days in much the same way as Thiesen. Lounging and flittering time away in sun-drenched locales across the universe. There was a wide range of gods, and a large portion never involved themselves with the constant power struggles, until now.

Without Forseti, leisure wouldn't be possible. If their peace were to end, then they became as vulnerable as the multitudes they needed to protect.

"No, he's the same asshole. Though a bit more gruesome than I remember. Things are progressing past what can be explained, and we need answers."

"What do you suggest?" Agomon asked.

"Go on the offensive."

***

The branches clung to Net and tore at her dress, but she continued pushing forward through the dense underbrush. The full moon shone bright, lighting her way. Every night this dream returned, and every night she'd get a bit farther along the path on her way to somewhere. The leaf-covered trees were welcoming, but the path held hidden dangers for her bare feet. Sharp stones, fallen limbs, and rough, tangled grasses hurt, and she was positive she was bleeding again, though every morning she woke with unmarred skin.

She had no idea if it were customary for mortals to have recurring dreams, and she wondered if all mortals' dreams were this vivid, this real. It had been over a month since she'd seen Fenrir, and thankfully no one had tried to break through his protective barriers since.

Of course, she didn't wish for another attack, but the prospect of seeing him again was alluring. Daydreaming about the wolf god had become a favorite pastime. She chided herself for spending any time mooning over a soul so damaged by the loss of his mate that he never shifted back to a man.

"Ouch." Deep in her dream, she stopped to pull a thorn from her heel. Was she a glutton for punishment? Was that why she walked down this same path every night, or was it part of her punishment? The similarities to the tale of Sisyphus and his uphill boulder rolling issue had not been lost on her.

She hadn't had a good night's rest since Fenrir left. She dreaded going to sleep, and often caught herself dozing in the middle of the day from exhaustion. This mortal existence was so unlike being a goddess. Tired, irritable, cranky, hungry, unable to focus were all states of being unfamiliar to her, and Net didn't like any of it.

Her dream was quickly turning into a nightmare, and she wondered if the same creature would come lunging out at her tonight.

Tonight, she managed to walk a bit farther along the path and closer to something she could feel was essential to her understanding of why she was here, but then the same beast came out of nowhere and attacked her, causing her to scramble awake. As always, she found herself lying in her bed, safe inside the cottage.

She got up, made herself a cup of tea. Sat on the sofa and stared into the dark, trying to figure out the meaning of the recurring nightmare. Every time she thought she was getting close to an answer, a horrific beast attacked her, and she woke immediately.

The tea had done its job, and Net leaned against the soft cushion and wrapped the throw around her. Her lids drooped, and she didn't fight the pull. She was back in the dream, wandering the forest, following the path. This time she continued on past where she'd left off earlier. She kept up her vigilance as she prepared for the inevitable attack. But, for the first time, it didn't come. A large stand of trees barred her way, and she struggled to squeeze through their tight, thick branches and trunks.

The bark tore at her skin, but she pushed on until the dense foliage began to thin. It was only on the other side that she realized if she'd crawled, it would have been a lot easier. The branches thinned near the bottom. She'd have to remember that if she made it this far again.

Gasping for breath, she broke through into a clearing. With her hands on her thighs, she sucked in the fresh, crisp air. She'd made it through, but she was uncertain as to where.

Sensing that she was no longer alone, she stood straight to face the danger head-on. She may be mortal, but she wasn't a coward.

Instead of impending danger, she saw a man on his knees chained to the ground. She attempted to go to him, but her feet were rooted.

When the man finally raised his bowed head, she was shocked to see who it was.

"Forseti?"

Chapter Three

Net jackknifed awake on the sofa. Fear and confusion warred inside her. She threw back the throw to find evidence that she wasn't crazy.

"Fenrir," she called, and her bracelets warmed immediately.

She touched the dirt and twigs covering her bare feet to be sure what she was seeing was, in fact, real.

The air beside the sofa shimmered before Fenrir appeared. He looked from her to her dirt-covered feet. "You're bleeding again."

Net was well aware of the cuts on her feet, but they had more significant concerns. "I saw Forseti."

Fenrir's big wolf head tilted slightly. "What?"

"I saw Forseti. I've been dreaming of walking in the forest and a beast attacks me, but last night my dream, which," she held up her foot, "may not have been a dream, led me to Forseti, who was chained to the ground," Net explained, hardly believing it herself.

Fenrir tilted his massive wolf head, and since she couldn't read wolf expressions, she figured he didn't believe her. She hardly believed it herself. "Let's take a look at your feet first. Then you can explain to me why you would be walking outside without shoes on in the middle of the night."

"Listen to me." She stopped his movement. "I've been having the same dream for a month, and this is the first time I woke up knowing why. I woke up here, so I don't know why it looks like I was wandering around in the middle of the night. I can't explain that. We have to find Forseti."

Fenrir looked at her for a moment longer before saying. "Before we go over this in detail, let me heal your feet."

"Okay. Thank you." The pain ceased immediately, and she had to admit she felt better.

"Now, tell me everything," Fenrir requested.

***

Fenrir listened as Net recounted her dreams. At first, he thought perhaps she'd been sleepwalking. It wasn't uncommon for mortals to do so. However, the detail with which she was able to describe the beast that attacked her night after night was eerie. Its existence was known only to a select group of gods, which made the sleepwalking theory unlikely.

A Writhen was a beast leftover from when all existence began. Its razor-sharp, foot-long talons curved like sickles, enabling it to inflict untold damage with every strike. Its jagged beak, used to punch and tear its victims apart, was lethal. Spikes along its back jutted out in all directions and served as a deadly battering ram.

Its six eyes rotated independently of one another, enabling it to have a three-hundred-sixty-degree sightline, leaving the beast impossible to sneak up on and attack. Coarse, almost impenetrable, brown fur covered the remainder of its body, making it the perfect weapon.

"So, what do you think?" Net asked while picking the remaining twigs and stone off the sofa.

"Why didn't you call for me when these dreams began?" he asked. The thought of her suffering for a month with nightly attacks by a Writhen had him growling in the back of his throat. When he found the owner of the beast, Fenrir would delight in turning the beast on its master before eliminating it from existence.

Net looked away and said, "At first I thought these types of dreams were normal for a mortal, but as the nights wore on, the images and physical damage became more realistic. It never occurred to me to tell you about dreams. Until now, I had no proof, and nothing more than nightmares. I didn't want to pull you away from protecting the packs. They are the ones who are truly in danger."

She put herself below others in importance, which was uncommon for a god, making Fenrir marvel at her compassion. Net wasn't anything close to resembling most of the gods he'd encountered over the countless years of his long life.

"You are important to me. I want you to know that you can contact me for any reason," he told her. "I shouldn't have left you here alone for so long. That will change immediately."

Net looked at him from beneath her long lashes, almost as if she didn't want him to know what she was feeling. She had to know he sensed her emotions and scented her attraction. "Okay."

Fenrir got up on the sofa and stretched out, his head near her knee. "I believe there's more going on here than a random dream repeating itself. Forseti is trying to reach out to you."

"Me?" Net barked out a laugh before crossing her arms. "He hates me. Why would he want to contact me?"

"He doesn't hate you," Fenrir stated. "He was misguided and harsh in his judgment, and there's more to that than I know, but regardless, he doesn't hate you."

"You could have fooled me," she muttered.

"He was a grieving father when he lost Bain, and you hired a Reaper to dispose of someone you viewed as a rival."

Net leaned back against the cushions with a huff. "I grieved too, but that never mattered to Forseti. As for hiring a Reaper, I was not myself, and upon realizing what I'd done, I went to protect its target."

"You did," Fenrir agreed. "That is why your sentence wasn't permanent."

She gave him a *we'll see* look. "Let's say for a moment you're right. Why would Forseti set the beast on me if he wanted my help?"

"I don't believe the beast is under his control. The being responsible for Forseti's disappearance may be trying to keep you away. You turned out to be more determined than they'd expected, making it farther each night."

"That could be possible, but I still don't know what he wanted from me. It's not as if I have any power to help him. He better than anyone knows that."

"Ah, but as a mortal, your mind is easily accessed. He knows that, and probably figures once he reached you, you could bring help."

"That makes sense," she said. "I could go back to sleep and try to reach him." The thought held no appeal for him. Sending her back into that dream was the last thing he wanted her to do.

"I'm not a fan of that approach. Now that the beast's master knows you avoided it and reached Forseti, a return is guaranteed to be worse than anything you've experienced so far." Net rubbed the palms of her hands down her face.

Fenrir hadn't missed the dark smudges under her beautiful but bloodshot eyes. "I will stay with you while you sleep. If I sense you suffering, I will wake you to end the dream."

"What if it's not a dream, and I get sucked into wherever it is? Remember, I woke up with bloody feet with leaves and twigs stuck to them."

Fenrir didn't forget that for one moment. "You're anchored to me." He tilted his head toward her bracelets. "Wherever you are, I can find you instantaneously."

"Okay. I'll try," she agreed. "The worst part was being alone after waking from the dreams. Having you here will be reassuring."

Fenrir hated that Net was lonely, but the world outside this bubble wasn't safe for her without her powers. Even inside the bubble, she didn't seem safe. Beasts attacking while Forseti beckoned.

She yawned wide and covered her mouth with her hand.

"Perhaps you should try going back to sleep now. It's still hours before dawn." Maybe they'd get lucky and uncover the truth tonight so she would be free of the dream, and they might find Forseti.

"You'll be right here?"

"I swear to be by your side until you wake." He would never break a promise to her. Over the centuries of her isolation in the forest, he'd visited her often, and they'd grown close.

The irony of that statement hit him. Net had spent centuries under a curse set upon her by her brother. Spending those centuries alone in that damn forest was what Fenrir was forcing upon her now, only with better furnishings.

How was he only realizing this now? "I'm sorry."

She scrunched up her nose. "Why would you feel the need to apologize to me? You're the closest of all beings I have. You have helped me at every turn. We're friends."

Yes, friends. But they were more. That he'd started to realize it only recently made him feel foolish. He'd lived a narrow and bitter existence since his mate died. He never considered there might be more to life than sorrow and duty. Another correction he intended to make. For now, though, he'd be her anchor in more ways than one. Starting with getting her through her dream.

"I have you prisoner here, same as Vengier had with his curse. You are alone and justifiably lonely going through a major upheaval in your life. I should have visited more often and arranged for others to come visit you. I know Katrina, Lily, or Helena would enjoy visiting with you."

Net slid forward and before he realized her intent, she wrapped her arms around his fur-covered neck.

When she pulled away, their gazes met, and he had the overwhelming sensation that she could see straight through to his core. Which, of course, she couldn't. Not now in her mortal state.

A tear slid down her cheek as she ran her small hands through his neck fur. "You have nothing to be sorry about, Fenrir. I prize our relationship above all others and will continue to do so for the remainder of my days." Net's head drooped a little, probably due to exhaustion.

"Your eyes are closing as we speak. Do you need something to drink before lying back down?"

"Perhaps a glass of water. In this mortal form, I'm perpetually thirsty." A glass materialized on the coffee table. "Thank you," she said before taking a long sip.

She pulled the throw over her, and buried herself deeper into his furry coat. Her hand absently stroked his fur as her warm breath moved the fur on his face.

Now more than ever he began to believe Net could be his mate, that he did deserve a second chance. He hadn't been able to protect his mate, but he was protecting Net. Those bracelets were a tether, and he had no intention of letting her go.

Her breathing evened out, and soon she was fast asleep. Fenrir would remain alert to any signs of stress or fear, and pull Net out of her dream immediately or follow her to where the dream took her.

He would not fail her.

***

Net looked at the path before her with disdain. "Can't we simply skip this part and start where I left off?"

The resounding silence was her only reply, so off she went, yet again. The same branches clung to her as before, and the same damn thorn buried itself into her heel. Net was careful to keep her emotions in check. She didn't want to cause Fenrir to wake her too soon, not before she'd had a chance to make it back to Forseti and find out what he wanted her to do. Considering she was mortal, she didn't expect a lot. Maybe deliver a message at best.

The familiar wall of trees stood before her once again. She'd found Forseti on the other side of it, so she got down on her knees and crawled, pushing her way into the foliage. The sting from the sharp branches as they raked across her skin made her hiss, but this time she held that pain in tight. She could do this. Net had to make it to Forseti and figure out how to help him, or everything she'd gone through would be in vain.

When she reached the opposite side, she didn't bother resting to take a breath as she'd done last time. Instead, she stood and ran straight for the man in chains.

She slid onto her knees in front of Forseti and gently lifted his head. Multiple wounds covered most of his body, including his face, but his eyes were steady as they stared at her.

"How can I help you?" she asked.

"You made it through the forest," he said with a dry, raspy voice. "How?"

"I've been walking around this forest from hell every night for over thirty days. I was bound to find a way to you eventually, or it could be dumb luck."

"You are the only one who has made it to me," he remarked. "Perhaps I've judged you too harshly." His statement confused her. Had he called others for help?

"Later. The beast should be showing up any time now." She would prefer not to be here when that happened.

"Yes, before the Writhen returns. Hold out your hands," Forseti instructed.

She didn't know why, but she trusted that he knew what he was doing. A small, glowing orb appeared in the palm of her right hand, and she instinctively covered it with her other hand to hide it from sight.

"You must swallow the orb," Forseti explained with difficulty. He appeared to be getting weaker with each second that passed. "It will protect you while leading you to me."

Net looked down at the sizeable ball. "Swallow it? How?" *Really?* It was the size of an apricot pit. "Is there water somewhere?" By the looks of the dry, cracked soil, Net doubted it.

"No, do it quickly," he ordered.

"Can you at least tell me who did this to you?" she asked, but the ferocious roar of the Writhen filled the clearing with bone-chilling terror. "Shit, time's up."

When she looked past Forseti, she saw the Writhen less than a hundred yards away from them and closing fast. Time was not on her side.

"I will find you, Forseti, I swear it," Net said before swallowing the orb only moments before the Writhen reached her. It was amazing what a person would be willing to do when staring down a raging beast.

She screamed, but its claws never reached her. One moment she was face-to-face with the monster, and the next, she was waking up in the strong arms of a man. *Arms?*

She looked up into a pair of panicked pale blue eyes and said, "Hello, Fenrir."

Chapter Four

Fenrir felt odd in his human form. It had been centuries since he'd shifted back, but now being with Net as a man felt right. He'd had difficulty waking her, and when it became apparent she was in distress, to get a better hold on her flailing body, he was forced to change to man.

"Hello, Net. Are you well?" he asked before tearing away the throw and checking her for any possible wounds.

Those jade green eyes were trained on his face, no matter how he twisted and turned her while checking her over. "I'm fine. No pain at all, but I guess that's what Forseti meant by protection."

"You spoke with Forseti?" He knew she'd make it. She was one of the most determined women he knew.

She raised her hand and traced his brow with her fingers. "I've waited a long time to meet this side of you."

Fenrir couldn't stop himself from leaning into her soft palm as she cupped his face. "I've not been in this form for quite some time."

"Not that I'm complaining, because I'd love for you to stay this way far more often than you do, but why?" she asked, and for a brief moment, she allowed her emotions to show.

"You needed me," he replied quickly. "I had to wake you, and my wolf wasn't having any luck doing that."

"You did this for me?" she asked.

"Yes. I would do anything for you." Perhaps he'd never made that clear. He knew he wasn't the best at communicating how he felt.

Her hand drew him closer to her face. There wasn't a chance he'd fight the draw to kiss her finally. When their lips met, a deep groan reverberated up through his chest. Her soft lips molded to his own as their tongues explored the depths of their mouths.

He deepened the kiss and placed his hand behind her head, holding her where he wanted her. Her responding moan assured him she welcomed his attention. He pulled her even closer to his naked body. Her silk tank top and shorts slid across his skin, adding to the erotic sensations running through his body.

Their legs intertwined as all space between them disappeared. Fenrir hadn't taken a woman into his arms in centuries, and now that he knew what it felt to have Net pressed tight against him, he knew he'd never let her go.

Her nails raked over his back, adding a new level to his desire for her. He carded his fingers through her lustrous blonde hair before taking hold and pulling her head back so that he could continue his exploration down her neck.

Her quick intake of air drove him on as he kissed, nibbled, and sucked, all the while fighting the urge to bite her, sealing their bond. He imagined she would require more time to accept this change in their relationship, and he wouldn't push.

Those soft moans were progressively becoming louder, fueling his passion. If he was being honest with himself, he'd wanted her for decades, and finally getting what he'd secretly desired, he'd treasure this moment long into the future.

Suddenly alarms began sounding, causing them to break apart. Damn timing couldn't be worse, but he had to deal with whoever had come knocking.

"Let me see who that is," Fenrir growled. "I'm sorry."

Net's pupils were blown wide open. Her swollen lips and the beautiful flush on her face served to make his regret stronger.

"Of course. I'll get dressed," she said before rolling off the sofa and heading to her bedroom.

Fenrir shifted back to wolf and jumped off the couch on his way to the front door. Whoever this was had better have a damn good reason to be here, or else they might not make it out of here alive.

***

Net couldn't stop her racing heart no matter how hard she tried. Their intense kiss had left her happily confused. Of course, she wanted him, but she never imagined the feeling was mutual. She'd assumed he wouldn't accept her advances and long ago decided to cherish their friendship instead.

Good to know she was wrong.

Another blast vibrated the cottage, making her pull on her jeans faster. Who the hell was it now? She was done with uninvited guests. She pulled up her zipper and buttoned her top as the early morning sky filled with flashes of light and explosions. There would be more damage to the cottage because whoever was out there surely was here for her.

Her hands shook with rage. Fenrir was out there fighting them alone. The next tremor smashed the window beside her and jarred the wooden beams above her. Before she had time to react, the timbers let loose, plummeting down on top of her.

She closed her eyes and waited for the impact knowing that this would be more than enough to kill her mortal body, but it never came. She cracked one eye open to find the beams strewn across the bed and floor of her bedroom. A golden glow surrounded her body, reminding Net Forseti had her swallow an orb. So this was what he meant by protection. She hoped the protection extended to any threat hurled at her.

The front door banged opened, and Fenrir raced inside. He took one look at the room and her with her new glow and asked, "Forseti?"

"Yes," Net answered while poking her finger through the translucent barrier. Her fingers went through, but none of the wood had gotten in. "I wonder how I control it, and if I spread it to other people." If she could, she'd wrap it around Fenrir in a heartbeat.

"I'm thrilled you have it, but we'll figure it out later. We have to leave. There are too many of them. Whatever you've accomplished tonight with Forseti has upset those interested in keeping The Judge's location a secret."

Net was surprised they'd known so quickly and they'd found her. She ran to Fenrir and held on to his fur as he teleported them away from the place she'd called home for over a year. She was happy to be free from her seclusion and sorry to be leaving the cottage behind. It had served as the first home she'd had in what felt like an eternity.

"We'll return and rebuild it together." His voice surrounded her as they flowed among the different streams of life on their way to a safer location, although she feared it would be temporary.

She embraced the feeling of the forces around her. She'd lost that ability with her sentence and soaked as much in as she could. It always warmed her to be part of a larger universe. She missed communing with her fellow gods.

She held on tighter to Fenrir's wolf when she felt four other gods flanking them. Oh no, their attackers caught up with them.

"Don't worry. They're with us," Fenrir explained.

"This is the team you told me about."

"Yes. They're escorting us to a well-hidden location where you will be safe."

Net doubted she'd ever be safe again but kept that thought to herself. First, Forseti took her powers, and now because of some orb he gave her, more malevolence was after her. Great. *Sure, he doesn't hate me, right.*

The air grew colder, and she couldn't hide the shivers that raced through her body. As a mortal, she now felt when the climate changed around her. Before she had a chance to shiver again, a thick coat surrounded her in its warmth.

She snuggled further into his thick, warm fur and moaned her thanks.

"We are almost there. It won't be much longer," he said.

Net felt each time they changed directions. Probably a ruse to keep whoever was following them off their scent. They began slowing as rough terrain came into focus. Sharp cliffs and jagged rocks covered wherever they were as an ocean battered a sheer rock face. She admired the wild beauty for only a moment before they "landed" inside a massive cave.

The cold limestone burned her bare feet. She'd run out before she could put on her shoes. Fenrir blinked and boots appeared on her now-socked feet, and a long woolen sweater appeared over her tank top.

She was about to thank him when the whole cave lit up from within, bringing along a welcoming warmth. A fire roared toward the center of the cave, leaving a trail of smoke drifting into the black nothingness above them.

Throw rugs covered the limestone, and she recognized the patterns. They were identical to the ones she'd placed throughout the cottage. Her bed, or one identical to it, appeared on a flat ledge a few yards away along with one of the living room chairs and the coffee table. It was as if parts of the cottage were reappearing here in the cave.

"When we have the time, I'll add more necessities to make you comfortable," Fenrir explained as she watched her colorful pillows appear on the chair and bed.

"This is amazing," she whispered. "Thank you."

She ran her fingers through his fur as she took in her new home. With the addition of light, warmth, and furnishings, it wasn't so bad, and a hell of a lot better than the other option.

"You're welcome," he replied. "I must go talk with the team to ensure your continued safety. Perhaps afterward, we can discuss what you learned from Forseti."

"Why didn't they come inside with us?"

"This is your private domain. They know better unless invited."

Translation: He didn't want anyone in here with her but him.

She smiled and ran her fingers through his ruff. "If we're all working together to find Forseti, let's invite them in now," Net suggested.

Fenrir bowed his large wolf head and said, "All right."

"I'd like to meet them, and they need to trust me."

Several feet away, the air shimmered moments before the four other gods appeared before her.

"Agomon, Theisen, Meruim, and Abba, this is Net." As he said their names, in turn, they nodded except the female, who scowled. "They are helping in the search for Forseti and the return of balance in all the realms."

Agomon stood tall and strong, a warrior through and through. Theisen looked bored, and Net imagined he spent his days indulging in his interests. Doing this had to be a stretch for him. Abba sat on a nearby boulder taking everything in, and Meruim's animosity came off her in waves.

Net remembered Meruim. The two of them had a run-in centuries ago, and it appeared the goddess was holding a grudge.

"Hello, everyone. Thank you for coming to help me."

"I'm not here to help you, oh Divine Mother Nature. I couldn't care less about what happens to you. All we want is for things to return to normal, and if you're the way to achieve that, then fine, I'll help," Meruim said without trying to hide her disdain.

Fenrir growled and took several steps toward Meruim, but Net held him tight. They needed as many allies as they could get. Even this foul woman.

"Meruim," Net began. "It's been centuries. Surely, time has erased whatever we felt at the moment."

"You got in my way. I would have had my father's legions defeated if you hadn't stuck your nose where it wasn't invited." The goddess could barely control her rage.

Net let out a deep breath. Meruim would never change. She had spent centuries battling her father over some offense. Net doubted the two of them remembered what had begun the family feud, but there was no way Net would've allowed the kind of destruction Meruim had intended.

"You set fire to an entire forest. The creatures that made that forest home would have been burned alive. You and your father cause enough destruction when you are anywhere near each other. I could not allow you to destroy an ancient forest in an attempt to draw out your enemies." Such a disregard for life was appalling.

Meruim didn't look as though Net's words had registered with her. The same anger and hatred shot off her like shards of bright light.

"It was none of your business," she growled.

"I beg to differ. Remember, Divine Mother, Mother Nature, goddess of flora and fauna. Ring any bells?" Net knew she'd done the right thing. She made the skies open and pour down rain onto the flames, dousing them immediately.

"You and I should stay far apart," Meruim stated.

"Agreed." Who'd want to be close to this goddess?

"Can we please get on with the Forseti issue?" Thiesen asked, leaning back against the wall. "What have you learned?"

"Forseti has been in contact with Net."

At that declaration, all four looked over at her. "I spoke with Forseti through a dream."

"A dream. Right." Meruim's dismissive tone wasn't a surprise.

Not only did Net have to deal with demons, a Writhen, and traitorous gods, now she had an ill-tempered goddess to tiptoe around. She hoped they'd find Forseti before everything imploded.

"If you're going to whine, leave," Abba growled. "You're not helping matters, and at this moment we can't afford for you to turn into a risk."

Meruim turned to face Abba. "Did you just call me a risk?"

"Your antagonistic behavior risks us all. Your mind is consumed with anger. Instead of calmly dealing with your issues, you're liable to go off at any moment. Therefore, you make yourself a risk to us and our mission."

Instead of blowing, as Net had expected, Meruim took a deep breath and said, "So this dream of yours."

Net took a seat on one of the many cushions lying on top of a large flat rock. "I've been having a recurring dream that leads me into the forest. Every night I'd get a bit closer to what I assumed was my destination before a Writhen attacked."

"A Writhen? I haven't seen one of those in millennia," Agomon stated. "Are you sure?"

"Net described the beast down to the last detail. Definitely a Writhen," Fenrir answered as he joined her on the rock.

"When I finally made it through the trees," Net continued, "I found Forseti chained to the ground in a clearing. He said I was the only one who'd made it to him, so I assume he contacted more gods. He gave me a small orb and asked me to swallow it. Since the Writhen was bearing down on me, I did what he said."

"What's the orb supposed to do?" Abba asked.

"Lead us to him and protect me while we try to reach him," Net explained.

"Protect you, how?" Meruim asked, giving Net an idea.

Net looked at Fenrir before saying to Meruim, "Throw your dagger at me."

Understandably, the three other gods rose and voiced their concerns. Fenrir sat stoically. She felt his concern about a sharp object hurtling her way, but he'd seen the glowing protection around her in the cottage. He understood she was safe.

Meruim pulled out her blade and, without hesitation, let it fly straight at Net's chest. The vicious woman was going for the death blow. When the dagger reached Net's shield, it ricocheted off and fell to the ground in pieces.

"Shit," Meruim growled. "That was a perfect shot."

Net shook her head. "Let it go and accept that we are in this together. After we get Forseti back, you can hate me all you want. We'll likely never see each other again."

"We may be forced to work together, but the moment we have Forseti, you and I are going to finish this."

"She is mortal," Fenrir reminded Meruim. "You will have to wait until she has her powers back, or you'll be dealing with me."

The smirk on Meruim's face disappeared. Going up against Fenrir was foolish. Few gods held his power and strength. He was one of the original gods and, as such, carried the power to deal with anything that happened in all the realms. Even though Forseti was the most powerful, Fenrir was a formidable foe.

"So, how will you know where to go?" Thiesen asked. "I'd like to get this over with as soon as possible." He held his hand up, inspected his fingernails, shook his head, and sighed.

"I don't know," Net admitted. "We didn't have time for a long discussion."

"Great, so we sit here and wait?" Agomon asked. The warrior god didn't look like the patient type.

"It's the best chance we have of getting to The Judge," Fenrir said slowly as if he were explaining this to a class of four-year-old shifters.

"Fine, call me when you get your radar fixed," Meruim huffed. "I'll be outside."

Net could feel the tension in the room dissipate the moment Meruim vanished. This hadn't been the way Net wished to begin things with the team, but vengeance was a powerful master, and Meruim was drowning in it. Net wondered if the other woman had been this way her entire existence.

One thing Net was sure of: she'd never turn her back to Meruim without expecting the blade of her sword to hit home.

Chapter Five

"She must die."

"Yes, master. It will be done, my Prince," his faithful servants eagerly agreed. Their claws clicked against the ground as they milled around him. Their reptilian eyes followed his every move. Half man, half beast, all deadly. His followers, demons one and all, had benefitted from their master's plan and remained loyal to him...for now.

Hellion paced the ground outside the forest of souls. He stabbed the heel of his boot into the earth with every step he took. His body was vibrating with anger, and he would soon need to vent it, but he'd wait for the right target.

"How did she make it in? No one can enter that forest. If they'd tried, their powers would be sucked dry, and they would be set upon by the Writhen."

No god could pass without facing sure death. Not even Hellion could set foot onto that soil. The closest he got was when he'd thrown his victims inside its dark recesses. Mainly lesser gods, beings, and creatures would be deposited into its dark recesses, and he'd walk away. Never once giving them a second thought.

Simply another soul to add to his collection. He was slowly siphoning off their life force and magic to maintain his powers. Hellion knew that without his forest, he was nothing, and he would defend it with all he had.

The fortunes were smiling upon him because he now had a true prize. A god worthy of his time and the provider of unimaginable power. As The Judge, Forseti had authority over all gods, but had never used this power to his advantage. His irrational moral code got in the way.

Hellion had paid a hefty price in order to capture Forseti. Nearly half his demon servants had been sacrificed while Hellion used almost all his power, cloaking the ensuing battle from the other gods. He didn't need them meddling in his hunt.

Now what he'd been trying to prevent was knocking on his front door. Gods were gathering in search of The Judge, and the powerless Goddess Net was leading them. He couldn't figure out how this happened. A goddess without a discernable power bested his Writhen. He swore the next time would be different. He'd place his entire stable of Writhens in the forest of souls if he had to. Forseti was never going to be set free.

Hellion was so close to completing his mission and refused to lose what he'd taken.

He'd send the ogres out to lure these so-called heroes to their deaths. Nothing would stop him when he was so close to his victory. He thought of the jealousy his associates would surely feel when he took over. A king didn't need colleagues, he needed power. Him, a part of a collective new leadership, was laughable.

As they bargained their positions within the hierarchy, he would bide his time and gather his strength. Before they even had a chance to suspect his true intentions, Hellion would have them on their knees bowing before him.

There was only room for one King of the Gods, and that was him. The sooner the others realized that, the easier the transition would go for them. Any who opposed his will would find themselves in the forest, nothing more than a power source for Hellion.

"Send out every hunter. Find Net and bring me her head."

***

Net rolled restlessly from her back to her side as sleep continued to elude her for the second night in a row. Strange images and feelings had her confused, frustrating her. The emotions weren't her own, and the images remained blurred, no matter how hard she concentrated.

Why couldn't Forseti have given her a map or a homing beacon? Net would settle for a simple direction. North, northeast, anything would have been better than nothing.

"I could command sleep upon you, if you wish," Fenrir suggested as he pulled her closer, offering her comfort in his arms.

He had been spending more time in his human form over the past few days. At night he'd shift, crawl into bed with her to hold her as she tried to sleep. Though she was thrilled to be held in his strong arms against his warm, hard body, sleep never came. Having him close was the best kind of distraction, but that wasn't why sleep eluded her.

Though she had wanted to pick up where they'd left off in the cottage, she was exhausted. Her mortal body insufficient to do the job of a goddess, and depleted from the lack of rest, her mind wasn't as sharp as it needed to be. If she concentrated on Fenrir, she'd sink into the pleasure of him, but there'd be nothing left for the critical mission at hand.

Duty before everything.

"No," she answered. "If I'm supposed to be awake to receive the instructions or direction, or whatever the hell Forseti wants when he gets around to telling me, being put in a deep sleep would be counterproductive."

"I'm sure he isn't trying to torture you. Perhaps it drained a large amount of his power to get you into the forest, and now he is resting and regaining strength for what comes next."

"I hate it when you're logical," she grumbled while pulling the comforter tighter around her neck.

The flames of the fire tripled in size, spreading warmth and lighting the cave's tunnels.

She hadn't said a word, but he'd noticed and had made certain she was comfortable. "Thank you," she said as she snuggled into his hard chest. "I think it's my lack of sleep that's making me feel so run-down and cold."

"You're worried you'll miss Forseti's call, and that's keeping you up at nights?"

"I don't know. Maybe subconsciously," Net said. "If I sleep right through his instructions on how to reach him, I'll condemn all the gods and worlds to an existence without justice." Imagine that tacked onto her name—Divine Mother, Destroyer of Worlds.

Fenrir rolled her over so that she could lay her head on his chest while he continued to hold her close. "You can't take all this responsibility onto yourself. You must share it with me. We are in this together. You aren't alone."

She wished she could, but she knew, in the end, it was all on her. "I can't help it. If I fail, the results could be catastrophic. I don't want that hovering over my head like a guillotine. One wrong move, and it will be my head in the basket."

He began rubbing circles across her back, helping to release a few of the knots that had been collecting in her sore muscles. She ran the palm of her hand over his muscled abdomen and up to the broad chest. She soaked in the peace and perfection of this one moment. How many would they have left? Her question was answered when Agomon appeared at the foot of their bed.

A growl worked its way up Fenrir's throat, making Agomon take several steps back. "There had better be a good reason for this interruption."

"Ogres are randomly attacking the packs. We need to join the others already fighting them off."

Net sat up, making sure she held the blanket in front of her body. Some gods weren't concerned with nudity. She was not one of them.

"You must go," she urged. "They need you." If one innocent life could be saved, Fenrir had to try.

He looked conflicted but shifted back into his wolf before answering. "I will be back as soon as possible. Stay in the cave."

"Don't worry about me. I have that shield Forseti gave me. No one should be able to harm me. Go, protect and save innocent lives."

Ogres were horrible beasts with their clawed hands dragging on the ground. Their disproportionately short legs and long torsos gave them a lumbering gait. Small heads on broad shoulders completed the gruesome picture of these bloodthirsty things.

Fenrir rubbed his muzzle against the side of Net's head before vanishing along with Agomon.

The fire still roared, but she was considerably colder than moments before.

***

Fenrir dodged another ax hurled across the clearing in his direction. Members of the Eastern Pines pack were hiding in bunkers hidden in the surrounding forest, leaving a contingent of gods and goddesses, as well as the pack's alpha, beta, and their warriors, to take on the beasts. The pack's powerful omega remained among their people to protect them if their defenses were breached. Ogres were indiscriminate killers. Women, children, and the elderly who couldn't fight, it didn't make a difference to them.

The earth shook with each ogre taken to the ground as they continued to fight even after losing limbs. The beasts were single-minded and did what their master ordered until they were dead. It wasn't uncommon to see some pulling themselves toward a battle without legs. The only way to assure they didn't keep coming was to take their heads.

While raking his claws across one beast's neck in an attempt to behead it, Fenrir brought lightning streaming down upon four others. Buildings burned as the battle raged. Homes, stores, and schools were all fair game in the ogres' onslaught.

Suddenly, someone summoned the rain to pour down and extinguish the flames, and for a brief moment, he felt Net's presence, but that was impossible.

Three packs were under attack, forcing them to spread their defenses thin, trying to hold the ogres back from destroying communities. More gods continued to appear in the fight, in answer to Fenrir's call for help.

However, a small number of gods came to aid the invaders instead, effectively declaring on which side of this dispute they were fighting. Some old misanthropes, who'd never held to their laws, had joined the ogres. Vengier came to mind. Unfortunately, there were a few familiar faces among them, which shocked Fenrir.

The Goddess Phume, fought side by side with the ogres, which caught Fenrir off guard. Centuries before, Forseti and Phume had once been lovers, and knowing she fought on the side of chaos, destruction, and death had caused Fenrir to wonder what could have transpired to make her turn on someone she professed to love.

Whatever it was, she had decided and was now his enemy. Fenrir sent a series of lightning bolts to strike her as she prepared to crush the pack's beta under a boulder the size of a small house.

The ensuing tremor knocked her off balance, causing the rock to come crashing down on top of her. She managed to vanish before it hit its mark. Fenrir transported the beta away before Phume had a second chance at him.

Phume reappeared steps away from Fenrir, her face etched with anger. "You fight for the losing side, wolf." Her warning flowed over him like a morbid caress.

"Wrong," Fenrir growled.

"We can rule over all of these inconsequential creatures," Phume hissed before flipping her black hair over her shoulders. "They would build temples and monuments to us on all worlds. We could demand sacrifices to earn our favor. Threaten them with floods, drought, and fire if they disobey. Wiping out a few packs is child's play and a reminder to the others of exactly who is in charge now."

Fenrir regarded the beautiful woman with the soul of a demon and laughed. He was infuriating her more with his flippant response, but he meant to goad her.

"You laugh at me?" she asked with a snarl as her hands began to glow. Her anger would be her undoing. "I hold your fate in my hands."

"I'd often wondered why your relationship with Forseti failed. Now I know why. No matter how much you flaunted your wiles, Forseti wouldn't be turned to your dark mind of how our existence should be. In the end, you were nothing but a cheap harlot. A trinket for his amusement."

"How dare you call me a whore," Phume screamed while raising her fiery hands high. Her eyes turned black as her innate evil took over.

Fenrir didn't even bother to move as Agomon tossed a headless ogre Phume's way, swiping her off her feet and carrying her hundreds of yards across the clearing.

The warrior nodded and carried on to the next attacker. With the increasing numbers of gods coming to their aid, the mob of ogres began to thin. Eventually, the few gods that were fighting with them began to abandon the battle, leaving the remaining creatures to their inevitable deaths.

Phume had taken off shortly after being pummeled by Agomon and hadn't returned, no doubt off planning her next attack. Over the next hour, the remaining threats were dealt with, and the fires extinguished. Fenrir tried to restore the town and community to its former beauty, but he knew no matter what he'd done, the scars of this battle would remain.

Pack warriors littered the ground while gods and goddesses raced to save as many as they could before true death took them. Theisen, Meruim, and Agomon joined him once those who could be saved were.

"The traitors gave up too easily," Fenrir stated.

"I thought the same," Thiesen agreed.

The other gods who'd come to their aid began to gather around. "Thank you to you all for coming to fight by our sides, brothers and sisters." Fenrir wanted them to know how much their loyalty meant to his people and all shifters.

"Do we have any idea where Forseti has been taken?" one asked from the back of the group.

"He has to be found," another stated.

The questions began, and Fenrir knew he'd have to be forthcoming if he wanted their continued cooperation. However, he despised having to put Net in the crosshairs for others who might use this information as a cause to get rid of her.

"Forseti has reached out to one of us for help," Fenrir said. "Net."

"The Divine Mother? I thought she was still under sentence and powerless." Goddess Lilliana said, but Fenrir didn't get the impression she was being cruel, only curious.

"Currently, she lives as a mortal." The words felt like they had been torn out of him. Anything that put Net in danger made him hyperaware of his surroundings and those in it. "Forseti came to Net in her dreams. I have seen the proof of this."

"So, Net is our only hope to return things to normal?" the goddess asked.

"Yes."

"Where is she?" another god asked from somewhere in the back. Fenrir couldn't see his face, but it didn't matter. He would never give away her location.

"We have her hidden in a safe place to wait for Forseti to reach out again. Once we have a location, we intend to find The Judge and free him." As imperative as it was to restore balance to all the realms, for Fenrir, keeping Net safe was paramount.

There was a murmur of discussions among the gathered gods. Fenrir was actively fighting his need to get back to Net this instant, and it was quickly becoming overpowering. In moments, whether the discussion was over or not, he was leaving.

Theros spoke up above the crowd. "The best way to ensure your team and Net are able to rescue Forseti is for the rest of us to take over guardianship of the remaining species of these worlds while you search."

Fenrir wanted to thank Theros for the offer but doubted the other gods would want to take time away from their responsibilities and leisure. That was until those others began speaking up and agreeing with Theros's idea.

"It's decided then. We, as a collective, will watch over the innocent beings of this world and all others until you find Forseti and free him. If you need further assistance, we will join you at that time."

"Thank you, all of you. This will surely help us find Forseti much faster. Many beings are suffering as our worlds deteriorate into chaos. We can't allow the innocent to be preyed upon."

"The Judge chose Net for a reason." One of the two jurors on Forseti's court, Mayal, stepped forward, her white hair ghosting behind her. She had been present at Net's sentencing. "It will become clear at some point."

"Net mentioned that Forseti claimed she was the only one who reached him. Perhaps there was more," Meruim said.

"I'd be curious if one of those gods was Phume?" Thiesen asked. "It would make sense why she'd left him where he's being held captive, the traitor."

"I must return to Net," Fenrir stated. "We will provide updates on our progress."

He didn't bother waiting for a reply before vanishing into the growing mist. There was a goddess he desperately needed to take into his arms to assure himself that she was indeed safe.

Chapter Six

Net cursed herself for going so far. Her feet were aching from trying to walk over the uneven and rocky cave floor. If she wasn't stubbing her toes, she was tripping over loose rocks. She couldn't imagine doing this without wearing the boots Fenrir had given her.

The short walk to clear her head had turned into an expedition as she wandered from one cave into another, trying to find the one she'd initially started from. She had been so consumed with worry over the battle she knew was being waged that she'd lost track of the direction she'd come.

Of the many thoughts swirling around her head, when had she fallen so profoundly for the wolf god had been at the forefront of her mind. She'd known she had feelings for Fenrir, but now she realized how deep those emotions ran.

At one point during her meandering, she felt the overpowering urge to summon the rain to pour down. She held on to that need and attempted to make it happen, but no matter how hard she concentrated, not so much as a drop spit from the sky, reconfirming that while Forseti's orb protected her, it lent no push to her powers.

Why he couldn't have ended her sentence so she'd be able to protect herself while searching for him was beyond her. The protective shield was a good defensive mechanism, but the orb did nothing to enhance her fighting abilities.

The flashlight in her hand had already blinked a couple of times, making her worry that the batteries were probably drained. When she asked Fenrir for one, she hadn't thought to specify endless battery life. He'd left a chest that worked on the same principles as the cupboards in the cottage. If she asked for something, it appeared. She'd have to be more specific with her requests.

Fenrir wasn't going to be happy about her getting lost. She felt stupid.

Water dripped down along the rock faces in various locations, and Net could hear rushing water somewhere close by. She wasn't frightened. She knew Fenrir would eventually find her. She decided to try to make productive use of her time and freedom among the various rock formations. By scouting the fullness of her surroundings, she could better protect herself. Being in a new environment presented a challenge, and she needed the distraction.

Stalactites hung from the ceilings in multiple caves, and stalagmites the size of tree trunks rose from the ground. The earth mother in her found the caves and their various formations stunning, making her miss her connection with the natural world around her even more.

As the Divine Mother, Net loved creation and life in all its forms, even here beneath the surface. Crystals twinkled everywhere her flashlight shone. Brilliant whites, purples, and blues dotted every wall and grew more numerous the closer she came to the source of the water.

Her connection to nature washed over her like a wave when she walked through a small tunnel that opened up into a giant cavern filled with even more crystals of various shapes and sizes, which ran along with an underground stream. A small pond veered off from the stream, creating an oasis of sorts beneath the earth. A wide crack in the rocks above allowed the moonlight to fill the space.

The cave provided an invitation to rest and lounge in this secluded spot. Net walked farther in to have a better look around. It shocked her that this part of the cave system was considerably warmer compared to the rest, making her exploration more comfortable. She turned off her flashlight and set it by the entrance, allowing the ethereal glow of the moon to light her way.

She couldn't stop herself from running her fingers over the sparkling stones, each a treasure hidden from the outside world. This place felt special to her—a garden of bright crystals and dark rock. For the first time since beginning her walk, she was warm enough to remove her coat.

The sound of her footsteps echoed into the far recesses of the cavern, breaking up the sounds of the flowing water. The area was full of life, but peaceful at the same time. She wished Fenrir were here to share in her discovery.

As if her hope had brought him to her, he appeared mere feet away, causing her to let out a small scream. "Give a girl the heads-up when you're about to pop in, wouldja," Net gasped out while trying to slow her racing heart.

"Why aren't you back in the original cave I prepared for you?" he asked, his concern evident in his tone. "Anything could have happened to you in here."

"Hi. Good to see you too," Net joked, trying to ease the tension. When he didn't respond, she said, "I still have my protection. No one could've harmed me. After you left, my mind filled with images of you in battle. I can't fight alongside you, and not knowing what's going on frightens me. I went for a walk to ease the stress."

"And promptly got lost?"

"Yeah, pretty much," Net grumbled. "But look what I've found." She waved her arms in the air to encompass the entire cave. "It's beautiful and warm. I like it here."

Fenrir shifted back into his human form, wearing only a pair of jeans, and gathered Net into his arms. "You have no idea how terrifying it was to return and not find you where I'd left you. Please, next time, wait until I return before you go exploring through the cave system."

Net could feel the fear radiating off him and felt terrible. "I'm sorry. I didn't mean to worry you." She hadn't done this to scare him. She'd been alone for an extremely long time and thinking about how other people would react to her whereabouts had, for the most part, fallen out of her thought process.

"I know you didn't," he said while brushing loose strands of her hair back behind her ears. "It took mere moments to find you, but they felt like hours."

She leaned into his arms and laid her head against his chest. The strong beat of his heart, combined with the safety and strength of his arms, lulled her into the warmth of security. One moment they were standing in the center of the cave, the next they were lying on thick fur blankets beside the tranquil pond she'd found.

"It's perfect here," she said through a yawn. "With you."

Those pale blue eyes seemed to be drinking her in. "I will never be far from you, Net."

Her eyes were getting heavy, and she struggled to get out her next word. "Promise."

"Oh yes," he rumbled, the sound radiating through the space.

***

The moon's glow had long faded, and the sun's rays streamed down in through the crack in the cave's ceiling. Net had no idea how long she'd slept, but there was no denying being held in Fenrir's arms, she'd had her best sleep in months. Her mind felt clear, and her body refreshed.

A splash caught her attention, and she looked over to find him swimming in the crystal-clear pond. She watched his hard body glide effortlessly through the water, propelled by his muscled arms and legs. She crawled out from underneath the covers and pillows, and began stripping out of her clothing so she could join him in the water.

As she approached the edge, he swam over to her, wearing nothing but a sexy smile.

"Good morning, beautiful. You had a restful sleep. How do you feel?"

She couldn't help but be distracted by the beads of water running down his strong jaw. "Like I'm brand new." She smiled. "It's amazing what a good night's sleep will do for a mortal body." She was having a new appreciation of how fragile mortals were and realized they needed to be protected. Always, she'd lovingly took care of her forests and its inhabitants, but now she had a greater understanding that many other creatures needed her protection, including shifters.

"Come in for a dip," he beckoned. "The water is warm." His arms spread out, causing steam to rise from the surface, and the temperature rose by several degrees.

She discarded the last bit of material from her body before responding to his suggestion, and dove in.

The water felt like silk against her skin, a warm caress from deep within the earth. She broke the surface to find him floating a few feet away, holding his arms open once again. Without a second thought, she swam into them and held him tight as their bodies intertwined under the surface.

"Tell me about the battle," she whispered, praying no one had perished, but knew that was impossible.

"For a species that supposedly died out centuries ago, there sure is a hell of a lot ogres still around," he grumbled. "Though something new did occur."

"I'm almost afraid to ask," she said.

"It appears as if a few gods have chosen to fight on the side of anarchy. Phume was among them."

"Forseti's lover?" That was one hell of a twist. Phume had professed her love and undying loyalty to anyone who'd listen.

"Not lovers any longer," Fenrir was quick to clarify.

"I was trapped in those woods for a long time. Last I was aware, the two were together. I gather the split wasn't amicable." Apparently, Phume had a score to settle.

"I'd often wonder why they'd parted, and now I believe I have my answer."

Net looked at Fenrir, and she had a feeling she already knew. "Forseti found out about her plans."

"I think Phume had tried to sway him to her way of thinking," he told her while brushing her wet hair off her face. "Clearly, it didn't work."

"I don't doubt Phume had a hand in Forseti's capture." Net had never been fond of the woman. Her ego was unmatched among the gods. Phume considered all other creatures to be beneath her. Once she'd secured a relationship with Forseti, she'd gloat about being the consort of The Judge.

"Exactly what I was thinking," Fenrir agreed. "Perhaps he let his guard down around her."

"That makes sense," Net said before her thoughts turned sad. "Were many lives lost in the battles?"

Fenrir took a deep breath before saying, "We managed to save all but four."

Every life was precious, though she had to admit she was glad to hear the forces of evil hadn't wiped out the entire pack. She wished she could honor the fallen. In the past, she'd have created an individual tree to symbolize each person lost. A new life added to the stream.

It had been a long time since she'd been able to do that. During the centuries she was cursed to remain in that forest, she hadn't been able to create anything. Her brother, that abomination Vengier, had found the worst possible means of torturing her. Instead of bringing life to flora and fauna of the forest, she sucked the energy away from them, killing the forest she loved for her brother's perceived sin of loving and mating a wolf shifter.

Fenrir and her brother had been at odds for millennia. Vengier, as he was wont to do, took their disagreement too far by attacking Fenrir's mortal mate, and caused her death. In the resulting battle, her brother was scarred when Fenrir raked his claw down Vengier's face.

After that, Vengier, the god of beauty, lost his mind and his soul to a deeper darkness than had lurked beneath the surface. His vanity was his undoing, and Net had thought she was finally free of him when he'd been torn to bits during the fight to free her from the curse.

Seeing those putrid pieces put back together was a living nightmare.

"Hey, hey, what's wrong?" Fenrir asked. "I can feel your stress and worry."

"Was my brother there?"

Fenrir's face turned solemn. "Yes. He was fighting alongside the ogres."

"Of course, he was. The man has never done the right thing ever in his pathetic eternal life."

She remembered once, when they'd been young, they were given a pet, a beautiful bird with wings of gold and a song as sweet as anything she'd ever heard. She'd cared for the creature every day until it went missing. Years later, she'd discovered that Vengier had been jealous of the attention the bird was receiving and had killed it. They were never permitted to have another pet after that.

Fenrir floated onto his back and pulled her up to lie on top of him. It was an impossible feat unless you were a god. His calloused fingers carded through her wet hair, stopping at her neck to rub away her tension.

"You are not responsible for him or his actions. None of us are."

"I was stripped of my powers based on my actions. I've wondered if I'm more like him than I thought." Fenrir shook his head and suddenly they were moving. When her vision cleared, they were back among the pillows and blankets.

"You know, you do that a lot. Ever hear of walking?" she groused playfully.

"My way is much more efficient," he replied before lowering his head to take her lips in a long, slow kiss. When they came up for air, he continued. "You are nothing like your brother. You were a victim of your brother's insanity. Every move you made after that was never your fault."

She thought over what he said while she continued to run her fingers through his chest hair. Those beautiful blue eyes kept careful watch. Perhaps he was right. She'd never hurt a soul before Vengier had cursed her. Before that, she'd spent her days among the forest and all its creatures, more concerned with creation than anything else.

"Have you ever wondered about the oddity of our relationship?" Net asked. She sure had.

"Oddity?"

She nodded. "My brother took my mate from me, but you saved him and allowed him to be reborn. Although he had no memory of me or what we'd shared, he has a life, and he's happy. My brother took your mate from you. Centuries later and here we are, like this." She raised her hand, gesturing between them. "I'm the sister of the man who hurt you so deeply. How can you stand to even look at me?"

At one time, she and her brother were similar in appearance. Both had golden-blond hair, pale complexions, and a tall build. While the basics remained the same, having lived through her brother's curse and cruelty, she'd changed. Not so much aged as wore her pain and regret. A shadow of her former self, especially without her powers, she doubted if she'd ever return to her former appearance.

Fenrir rolled over, pulling her on top of him. "You remind me of spring days, lush, fragrant flowers, tall trees, and pine. Your spirit floats along with the breeze from one wildflower to the next, and your heart blooms in all recesses of your beloved forests. That is what you remind me of."

She was struck speechless. Unsure of what to say, she laid her head on his chest. His warm hands stroked up and down her back, and the hard bulge pressing against her leg lent truth to his words and his feelings.

Adjusting herself slightly, she slid his cock between her thighs and flexed her hips in invitation. "Are we really going to do this?"

He cupped her face and in his deep, rich voice said, "I hope so. I treasure you, and have for a long time. We're meant to be together. The confluence of events that brought us to this moment gives us what we need, what we've been missing. There's no one else I'd trust to care for me as well as you." He dropped a kiss on her nose. "There's no one else I want in my arms."

She stroked his jaw and said, "Every single thing about you calls to me."

The distance closed between them, and their lips met once again. Their tongues explored as desperate moans filled the cave. Their bodies moved together as the temperature rose around them. He rolled them back into their original position, placing her beneath him.

He began to explore her neck to her collarbone, where he alternately ran his tongue and lightly ran his sharp teeth over the spot where he'd place his mating bite.

She arched into his touch as his talented tongue moved lower to circle her nipple before sucking the hard nub into his warm, wet mouth. His strong, calloused hands caressed her body as if she were the most precious of beings, making her feel cherished in a way she never had before.

Being mortal and having no power had changed their dynamic inside her mind. As a goddess, she always felt the need to be in control. Now, she was happy with him taking the lead. There was something freeing about not having to manage every aspect of her life. By giving away control, she was gaining trust she'd never enjoyed. The best part, if she wanted to take over, she knew her wolf would welcome it.

It was a heady feeling to have such a powerful being lavish her with such tenderness and care. To know the truth of her heart, that she'd come to love this man she hoped to call mate, was a revelation and a gift.

"I love you, Fenrir."

He slowed his movements and made his way back up her body. With a look of complete adoration, he said, "I love you too, Net. I have for a long time."

She wrapped her legs around his waist and pulled him in for a kiss. She could feel the head of his cock slide against her core.

"Make love to me. Mate me and make us one."

His eyes glowed as his wolf peeked through. A shifter, even a god, shared their existence with the animal part of themselves. Fenrir was equal parts man and wolf. The man did not hold power over the wolf, any more than the wolf held power over the man. They were one in mind and spirit.

Net wiggled her hips, making Fenrir's smile widen and the tips of his canines grow longer. Had anything ever been so sexy?

"As you wish, my goddess." Fenrir's voice was octaves lower than usual with a rough growl mixed in.

He took her lips in a punishing kiss while pushing the head of his cock forward, not stopping until he was buried deep inside her.

She broke the kiss and gasped for air as fire raced through her veins and pleasure poured over her. Every nerve ending was alive and electric, and she was desperate for more. Her legs intertwined with his once again as his hips flexed, pushing himself even deeper.

Her body was trembling with need as she flexed her hips in response. "You feel so good inside me."

His eyes glowed with power as his body poised over her. "I take you as my mate, Goddess Net, Divine Mother. My life and all that I am is yours as you are mine." His canines extended even farther. "With my bite, I seal my vow."

Then he struck, sinking his canines deep into the flesh above her collarbone. Leaving a mark that could only be removed by death as his hips began an erotic dance as old as time itself. The pleasure mounted as he licked his bite mark before rearing up and taking her with him.

With him sitting up on his knees and her mostly sitting on his lap, the angle changed, bringing her an entirely new set of sensations. Her moans mixed with her panting as her body began to tingle. The feel of his chest hair against her breasts spiked her need as their bodies moved in tandem, drawing out pleasure to the fullest.

Net opened her eyes, unsure when she had closed them, and found Fenrir watching her with a look of awe on his face.

"I love you, beautiful. I swear never to let anything harm you."

"We'll spend an eternity ensuring that, since I refuse to be parted from you ever again."

His smile melted her, and she moved in for another kiss. He brought his hand between them and used his thumb to rub against her sensitive clit, and that was all it took for her to be screaming out her release to the far reaches of the cave.

Fenrir's accompanying groan reverberated around them as Net collapsed against her new mate. A joy she'd been denied had finally returned, and she swore never to lose it again.

As they both gasped for air, his raspy voice broke the silence. "You are mine."

"And you are mine."

Chapter Seven

Net froze on the spot. She'd been making her bed when she heard it and felt the draw. The sheets hung from her hands as she concentrated. It was slight, but it was there, real and the first chance she'd been able to listen to him in the days since her last nightmare.

At first, he'd sounded like an insect buzzing around her ears, but when she stopped and paid closer attention to it, she could make out words or, more specifically, one word and an image.

"Are you all right?" Agomon asked from behind her, making Net jump and let out a small scream.

Once she'd calmed, she said, "You and Fenrir, always sneaking up on me."

Agomon smiled. Had he ever smiled before? He should do it more often because it took away the harsh lines on his face. "I didn't intend to, and had said your name before coming closer."

"Yeah, I was in my head, sorry. Something—"

Whatever she was about to say was cut short by an enraged Fenrir's entrance. Agomon took several steps away from Net, not wanting to get in the wolf god's way.

"You were scared. Who scared you?" he asked while shooting daggers at Agomon.

Net wrapped her arms around Fenrir's neck and kissed his jaw as he continued to glare at the other god. "I'm safe. No one hurt me. I was lost in thought and didn't hear Agomon call my name. When he came closer to get my attention, I jumped. He wasn't trying to scare me; he was concerned that I was staring off into space."

Fenrir's expression changed instantly. "I'm sorry for assuming the worst, Agomon."

Agomon laughed good-naturedly. "With the two of you being newly mated, I'm impressed you stopped to ask questions before attacking." It was a well-known fact that emotions ran high between a newly mated couple, and any perceived threat to a mate was removed with extreme prejudice.

Fenrir nuzzled his mating bite on Net's shoulder, sending excitement racing through her body. However, now wasn't the time to be distracted by more pleasurable pursuits.

"I was lost in my head because I heard Forseti in my thoughts moments ago," she shared.

Fenrir pulled back while the remaining two members of their team appeared. "Love, what did Forseti say?"

"It wasn't really words but a direction and an image. There's something there we need to find and bring with us." She knew it sounded far-fetched, but she was sure that's what Forseti meant.

"What is it?" Meruim asked.

"I don't know," she answered. "Forseti felt weak to me."

"We have to get to him before it's too late," Meruim stated the obvious.

"Agreed," Fenrir said. "The image he provided you, do you recognize it?"

"No, I've never seen this place before."

"Can you describe it to us? Perhaps one of us will," Thiesen suggested.

"Try," Abba added.

Net sat down on the bed and closed her eyes to concentrate on the image Forseti had shown her. "It's a dry area, pale sand with rock spires jutting toward the sky. There must be hundreds of them. Some thin, while others are wider than this cave. They have different colored rings with the darkest at the bottom of each spire, and the rings lighten as they go up."

She opened her eyes to find the other gods looking between themselves, all hopeful the description was enough to identify the location. At least they'd have a place to start, even if they didn't have a clue what they would be looking for.

"It could be the planes of Ezrelle on the red planet," Abba suggested. "I believe that those stone spires may be multicolored."

"There's a valley on this planet that also holds true to that description," Meruim stated.

Net looked at Fenrir and said, "How about we check the area out on this planet before trying another? I'll know the place when I see it, and perhaps by then, Forseti will have a chance to tell me what we're looking for." It seemed a logical next step.

Fenrir sat down beside her and took hold of her hand. "I don't like the idea of you out there without your powers, but I also accept that there is no other way to move forward. We'll begin with your plan, and if it turns out that neither are correct, we'll regroup here."

"It's the only way we're going to find him." Net stood, reached for her coat, and slipped it on. "The sooner we go, the sooner we get Forseti back." And maybe her powers.

Fenrir rose from the bed and stood beside her. "We follow your lead, love."

All six gathered at the center of the cave. Once they left their concealed shelter, Net would be out in the open once again. No longer could they tuck her away where no one could find her. Other gods would be able to sense her even if it was only slightly.

"I want Meruim and Abba to go on ahead and scout the area before I bring Net. Once you are certain this isn't a trap, contact us, and we will meet you there. If we run into hostile forces, we will scatter, and while you try to lead them away from Net, I will take her to the closest secure area."

"Try not to get yourself killed, Net," Meruim growled before disappearing, and Abba followed shortly after.

Net shook her head and said, "Always a pleasure, that one."

Fenrir held her close, as if at any moment she would disappear. She understood how difficult this whole situation was for them. He'd already lost one mate, and so had she. Given what was going on in all the realms, it could happen again.

She melted into his touch, soaking up as much as she could of what he freely offered. Someday she'd have her powers back, and he wouldn't have to worry as much as he was right now. Neither would she.

Net could admit that she was a bit anxious about going out into the open again and wished that Fenrir and her mating connection would kick in already. Sure, they were one hundred percent mated, but the ability to speak to one another through their own private link hadn't solidified as of yet. That worried her, but she, least of all, was in control of what would happen and when.

The warmth from his body calmed her jumpy nerves, though she would never admit to having them. Thiesen and Agomon flanked the two of them as they waited for word. Once the area was clear, they'd teleport to the first location. After leaving the cave with the skylight, Net had lost track of time, and day and night seemed to blend.

All three other gods tensed, and she knew they'd received a message. "Time to go?" she asked.

"Yes," Fenrir replied. "Meruim and Abba have searched the area and found nothing dangerous. It should be safe for us to travel. Are you ready?"

"As ready as I'm ever going to be." If they did nothing, Forseti would never be found and likely would not survive much longer. Net could feel The Judge fight against something or someone unknown that was draining him of his powers and life force.

Fenrir held her close, lowered his lips to hers before diving in for an all-encompassing kiss that left her gasping for air. "Stay safe." He stood back and shifted to wolf.

She wrapped her arms around his neck, and they were gone. This time when she joined the streams of existence, they were no longer peaceful but filled with anger, fear, and death. They had to find Forseti before there was nothing left to fight for. The cold air warmed the farther away they got from her cave, and soon she would no longer need a coat.

When they reappeared, they stood among towering rock formations. The sun shone down on her as the breeze lifted her hair from her shoulders. She removed her coat and laid it down on a nearby boulder. The ground was sandy, much like what she'd seen in her mind. The rocks spread in all directions, monoliths thrust from the soil, each a monument to the power of nature. They were stunning.

Net stepped forward to get a better look at the formations and to make sure they were the image Forseti had given to her. The colored bands on the rocks matched what she'd seen down to the last detail. Each red, yellow, orange, and brown were as vibrant as she'd remembered.

"Is this it?" Thiesen asked while keeping an eye on their surroundings.

Net had no doubt they were in the right place. "It is."

She continued walking forward in between two of the rock giants as the other four spread out. Fenrir stayed close by her side. There was an energy here. She could feel the surroundings calling to her for the first time in what felt like forever. The unexpected gift was a treasure after over a year of silence.

Kneeling, Net buried her hands into the hot sand, reveling in the connection. Fenrir must have felt her joy and wonder through their mating link.

"You can feel your life force communing with this area," he stated. "Odd, but not unwelcomed. Are you receiving any clues as to why we are here?"

Her concentration was disturbed by the high-pitched screech of a lone hawk circling the sky above them. Its broad wings blocked out the sunlight as it flew closer to them. All six went on alert. Net attempted to reach out to the animals of this world that she'd missed so much. She was shocked when she actually connected with the hawk.

It wasn't as if she could talk to the animals per se, even though she was the Divine Mother, but she received emotions and visions by way of communication. The hawk flew down and perched on a rock a couple of hundred yards away.

"He wants us to follow him," she said.

"How do we know it's not a trap?" Agomon asked.

"I sense no deceit. Only curiosity," she explained. "It's as if he has been waiting for us to arrive."

Fenrir padded up to her side, and Net dug her fingers into his fur. "I don't doubt you, so I guess we follow the bird," he agreed.

As if sensing their decision, the hawk took to the sky once again. Its dark brown wings reflected the sunlight as it rose ever higher.

"I can't believe we're listening to a bird," Meruim groused. "This is embarrassing. What's next, you going to commune with this beetle?" She raised her foot and stomped down on what most assuredly had been a beetle.

"You listen to Fenrir, and he's a wolf most of the time," Net pointed out, leaving her emotions out and using logic against the despicable woman.

Meruim shot her a withering look. "He is a god, not a dumb bird."

That earned her a growl from Net and Fenrir. "When will you learn, Meruim?"

"Learn what, exactly, oh Divine Mother?" Meruim sneered in disdain. Her anger and venom changed what could have been a vibrant, lovely woman into the sullen goddess.

Net calmly turned to face the disagreeable woman. "That every creature and being is connected. What you see as a *dumb* bird is a skilled hunter with speed and agility to rival even yours, and the eyesight to find its prey before ever getting close. It thrives in many different habitats and," Net stopped as the hawk began to glide closer to them before it dove lower still to leave a gift against Meruim's back. "And can spot an asshole equally as far away it would seem."

Meruim raised her hand toward the sky and at the hawk, preparing to send an arc of electricity straight at it. Before Net could think of how to stop her from killing the bird, the shield that Forseti had bestowed upon her expanded, effectively cutting Meruim's strike off before it had a chance to get near the majestic animal.

"Enough, Meruim," Abba shouted. Considering he was the quiet one of their odd group, it surprised Net to hear his raised voice. "I've sat back and watched you disparage everything and everyone. The anger inside of you burns anyone who tries to get near. You would kill the hawk leading us to something that could help us find Forseti and free him. Which brings me to wonder which side you are truly on."

"You doubt my loyalty. Are you challenging me?" Meruim growled, stopping in her tracks to face off with Abba. Net noted that Meruim had been itching for a fight since day one, perhaps missing the constant war she had fought with her father. However, this wasn't the time for petty differences.

Fenrir's response was swift and deadly, as he suddenly appeared between the two arguing gods. His wolf was substantially larger now, dwarfing everyone and everything in the area.

"This type of dispute will not be tolerated. We have what's left of our worlds to save, so check your egos and issues, or leave. There is no time for us to have to deal with this nonsense. After we get Forseti back, go at it, destroy one another for all I care, but for now, shove that shit down. Do. You. Understand?" Fenrir wasn't bluffing. His large, sharp canines were bared at them both.

Net watched as Meruim and Abba glared at each other once more before both backed down, though both kept exchanging hostile words.

"Fine," Meruim huffed. "After this is over, you and me, Abba, are going to go a few rounds."

"I look forward to it," Abba growled.

Net stood back, watching the hawk as it flew onward. The group was still arguing, and she'd had enough of this posturing, so she followed the bird. At least it didn't give her a headache.

As she wandered, Net began to feel the pull to something in the same direction as the hawk was flying. This had to mean whatever Forseti wanted her to find wasn't far from her current location. Excitement and trepidation grew with every step, and soon Net was farther away from her arguing team members than she'd intended to go.

Ahead was a grouping of three pure white rocks jutting toward the sky that sparkled much like the crystals had in the caves she'd explored. The sun seemed to make them glow brighter, and Net knew she'd found the right spot when the hawk landed on top of one of them.

"This is what you wanted me to see," Net said. "While it is stunning, how are these rocks going to help me find Forseti?" Yes, she was talking to the raptor. Though odd to others, to Net, it was all quite normal.

The hawk flew down onto the ground at the base of the rock formation and began scratching at a spot in the sand.

"Okay, I understand," Net said as she knelt. "Thank you for your help."

The hawk shook out his feathers before taking to the sky once again. A lone screech echoed around the rock formations long after the raptor was out of sight. Such a beautiful example of the nature around them.

She looked down at the spot in the sand where the hawk had scratched its claws and began digging. There had to be something hidden underneath that would aid them in their mission. After several minutes of finding nothing, she was concerned that Meruim might have been right, perhaps she was crazy following the hawk.

At the same time, she heard Fenrir calling her name, she touched a piece of cloth. She'd found something and pulled a small pouch from the earth, opening it to reveal a ruby pendant hanging on a lengthy chain. The same buzzing noise filled her mind, and Net had the overpowering urge to put it around her neck so that her personal shield would protect it. As she did, the ground began to tremble.

What now?

As she stood, Fenrir and the others came running around the rock pillars toward her from various directions. What she saw behind them was clearly impossible, it couldn't be real, but nonetheless a wall of water was bearing down on them fast.

Fenrir shifted and wrapped his arms around Net before taking to the sky and the tops of the rock formations. The water rushed in between the rocks filling the empty spaces until it reached the highest among them.

They bounded from the top of one rock to the next until they reached a large swath of land. Fenrir slowly released her as they watched the area around them transform and come to life. No longer a sand-covered patch of rock pillars, but as the water settled, islands emerged. The tops of the rocks were actually islands of various sizes as far as the eye could see.

Lush vegetation sprouted out of the earth at an accelerated rate. Trees grew, and flowers bloomed. Net felt as if she were dreaming of better times when she alone possessed the power to produce such natural beauty.

The sight was equally joyous and heartbreaking.

Chapter Eight

Fenrir could feel his heart pounding against his rib cage. He'd lost sight of Net for mere seconds, and she wasn't answering the calls he'd sent through their link. He wasn't even positive the link was fully working. Frantic, he sent his senses out into the valley for any sign of life. Once he'd located her, he was by her side moments later as the ground rumbled around him.

He held his mate out at arm's length, checking for even the slightest injury. "Are you hurt?"

"No, I'm fine," Net assured him. "I think I've found what Forseti sent us here to obtain."

He studied the ruby pendant hanging around her delicate neck by a silver chain and reached out to touch it. Net's shield quickly appeared, blocking him.

"You must remove that necklace at once," Fenrir growled. "You have no idea how dangerous it could be." It could be lethal, and there was no way he wanted it around his mate's neck.

"It's not harming me in the least," she replied as she ran her fingertips over the silver band the stone was set in. "I've never felt better."

"Then why won't your shield allow me to touch it?" he asked before trying again with the same result.

"Maybe it's so that no one can take it from me," she said. "Not even you."

Fenrir had to give this some thought. "The least we can do is look into it and check if someone knows what it is." There wasn't a chance he wouldn't discover its origin and power.

"Of course, we need to know what we're dealing with and how to use it. Do you think Forseti hid it here for me to find?" she asked, her expression hopeful. He knew it tormented Net to be without her powers. Having to be protected while still finding a purpose had to be infuriating. He couldn't have done as well, certainly by now, he'd be out of his mind from the imposed helplessness.

"I believe so," he agreed before pulling her back into his arms. Fenrir would never forget the fear he'd felt at her disappearance. "Why did you leave on your own?"

"The team's infighting was getting us nowhere, and the hawk was flying farther away. I didn't want to risk losing it while the others got their acts together," she answered while shaking her head at what he assumed was the nonsense of the others posturing.

"Please don't scare me like that again," he stated. "I tried to reach you through our link."

Her eyes widened in excitement. "I heard another buzzing sound in my mind, but I was digging where the hawk had scratched and wasn't concentrating fully. Maybe our link is finally settling into place."

"That could be, considering you'd heard nothing when I tried speaking to you earlier." He had to admit he was excited to share another form of intimacy with his mate.

Net smiled wide. "I hope so. It will be wonderful speaking to you no matter how far apart we are. It's comforting."

"To me as well, love," Fenrir said, not caring if others saw that as a weakness of the almighty wolf god. "Now, what do we know about the ruby?"

"The moment I freed it from the earth, the rumbling began, and then the waves of water came. It felt as if this area was returning to what it had once been and coming back to life because I'd removed the ruby from the ground."

Fenrir had to agree, it made sense. Whatever power the pendant held had to be strong enough to change the landscape. However, as long as it didn't hurt her, he would spend the time trying to figure out what was going on and why instead of trying to remove it from around her neck. Net's safety was first and foremost in all matters.

"Someone want to tell me what the hell that was?" Meruim's voice echoed from behind them. "I'm in a desert one minute and then a lush tropical forest the next. What gives?"

They both turned to find the four other members of their team looking around at the developing landscape in disbelief. It was as if an oasis had popped up in the middle of a desert, or in this case, hundreds of oases.

"Net has found what Forseti sent us here to recover, and I believe after that was accomplished, the area went back to its original form." Fenrir figured the abridged version would have to be enough for now.

Net held the necklace away from her skin to show the other four. "It was buried at the foot of a crystal formation." Fenrir knew she couldn't help herself, and she continued to say, "In the exact spot that the hawk led me to."

Meruim rolled her eyes and shook her head. "Whatever."

"So, what do we do with it?" Agomon asked while sheathing his glowing sword.

"I wish I knew," Net answered. "Forseti didn't bury an instruction manual with it."

"We should leave this place before we're discovered," Abba suggested while keeping a constant eye on the horizon. "An event this massive is bound to draw attention. Never know when those assholes will start showing up."

"Are we returning to the cave?" Net asked. "While the cave system is beautiful, do we have somewhere a bit more aboveground?"

"We won't be returning to the cave, my mate," Fenrir said. "We have a second location much closer that will keep you safe."

"We'll go on ahead and make sure it remains hidden from outsiders," Abba said as he and Meruim disappeared.

"Are you sure you want to leave those two alone after their squabble?" Net asked.

"If they can't be trusted, then they must leave," Agomon stated firmly. "There is no room for that type of distraction in a mission as significant as this one. Meruim is a given. Abba's reaction surprised me."

Considering Agomon came from a race of warrior gods, he knew the mission took precedence over everything else. His point of view made good sense. However, out among other gods, egos and emotions sometimes got in the way of cut-and-dry decisions.

"We will give them a chance to prove they can keep sight of the reason we are here," Fenrir answered. "We need all the help we can get at the moment." A levelheaded response was what was needed.

Moments later, they received the all-clear, and the lush new landscape faded away. Fenrir hoped this new location would make Net feel more at home.

***

Net was shocked by what she was seeing. The cottage or one that looked exactly like Fenrir's cottage stood only a few hundred yards away.

She looked up at him as tears gathered in her eyes. "You brought it here for me?"

"I know how much you loved our cottage, so I re-created it in this forest for the time being. When this is all over, I'll return it to where the original stood."

She wrapped her arms around his waist and hugged him close as tears streamed down her cheeks. She hadn't realized how much the cottage had come to mean to her until now.

"Thank you," she whispered. "This is what I needed."

She took hold of his hand and led him through the rows of thick evergreen trees and up to the front door of their cottage. The rest of the team had vanished, giving the newly mated couple some alone time.

While she and Fenrir were well aware of the need to discover the necklace's power and that they had to carry on with their search for Forseti, they needed a moment to be together.

When she reached for the door handle, Fenrir stopped her. Net looked up to find his expression one she'd never seen before, his cheeks were flushed, and he looked nervous.

"What's wrong, my love?"

He cupped the side of her face. "You have no idea what it does to me to hear you call me that."

"It means everything to me as well."

"I have a surprise for you, and I'm unsure if you'll like it."

Net couldn't contain her smile. She loved surprises. Well, good ones anyway. "Show me," she urged while pulling on his arm to enter the cottage.

"First, I'd like to do something I've witnessed my shifters perform."

Her curiosity piqued. "What is it exactly?" Her mind raced with possibilities, some on the racier side.

Fenrir bent and lifted Net into his arms, and with a nod of his head, the cottage door opened wide. "Apparently, in many cultures, it's a tradition to carry a mate over the threshold of their home the first time they enter as a mated couple."

Net lifted her face for a kiss that he gave without hesitation. "I believe in traditions. It's perfect."

He walked through the cottage and into the kitchen. The familiar warmth of home filled her with joy. Everything was as it should be with a few notable exceptions.

"What have you done?" she asked as he gently set her on her feet.

Everywhere she looked, there were items she'd chosen from either the enchanted cupboard or the chest in the cave. From her favorite throw blankets and pillows to her candles and flowers, it was all here. The silk scarves Net had requested from the chest and had used to hang as a barrier between their bed and the rest of the cave lay across the plush chair he'd given her. The art she'd chosen to brighten the space now hung among the others she'd placed on the living room walls before they were forced from the cottage.

She turned to find Fenrir watching her closely. A once irascible man who could do little more than growl had done this for her, and she loved him all the more for it.

"I love you, Fenrir. More than I can ever fully explain." However, that wouldn't stop her from showing him.

He crossed the distance between them and gathered her into his arms. "I love you, dear, sweet Net, and I'll be sure to remind you every day of how much."

He lowered his head and took her lips in a hungry kiss that led to an even deeper kiss, which led them to their bedroom, where Fenrir went about reminding her exactly how much he felt for her.

***

The breeze rolled between the towering trees as patches of blue sky appeared one moment to be covered with puffy clouds the next. Net lay watching the forest weave its magic from her perch on Fenrir's back. He was wolf, and given his size, she had no trouble laying herself on him to enjoy the warm day as much as she could while waiting for another sign from Forseti.

The forest floor was covered in moss, leaves, and branches. The pungent scent of damp, fertile earth filled her senses, making her relax even further. Colorful birds flitted between the trees, singing their joy for all to hear. The odd mouse and rabbit scurried out from the protection of one bush to go to the next.

She looked up and around her, taking in the various shades of green. The most renowned artist could never re-create the beauty and complexity before her. She itched to join nature's chorus with her vines and blooms. However, that was not to be, at least not yet.

"I miss being able to create," she spoke in a whisper, hoping not to disturb the tranquility around her. "To feel the ebb and flow of nature as if it were part of my own body. To breathe life into an area of desolation, bringing forth the blooms and growth in abundance."

"I know I can never fully understand your connection with the living world around us, but if I were forced to lose my connection with shifters, it would feel as if part of my body was missing." He laid his large wolf head on his front paws as if in reflection.

"That's exactly how I feel. A part of me is gone, and I grieve for its return. Now knowing that if anything were to happen to Forseti, my powers might be lost forever only serves to make me miss them more." She'd spent countless hours considering the ramifications to her and the realms if they didn't find Forseti in time. She would remain as a mortal, live a shortened life, and never be free to explore the worlds as she used to. An insignificant loss compared to what would happen when the balance of power remained unchecked.

"We will find The Judge, and you will get your powers back," Fenrir stated as if it were a forgone conclusion.

"We have to prepare for the possibility that I won't, love. Nothing is as it should be any longer. With Forseti as the only being holding enough power to pass judgment and impose sentences on the gods breaking our laws, it was only a matter of time before someone tried this. I've always believed that there should be a panel so that if the worst happened, our laws could still be upheld by the remaining members." The other two goddesses who had been present for Net's hearing were merely witnesses to ensure laws were upheld.

"How would you choose the panel?" he asked, and she could sense it was out of interest and not merely placating her.

She considered the question carefully before saying, "A test."

He turned so he could angle his wolf's head and look at her. "What type of test?"

She'd thought about this and quickly answered. "Perhaps one that judged how far a god would go to save an innocent life, although I'm unsure how that could be determined. However, if a god had an unwavering sense of the importance of every life, they'd be less likely to allow those who would abuse it to go unpunished."

"So, you're saying that the preservation of life should be the main qualifier?" he summed up.

"Absolutely. Without that, why are we here?" Net had thought this out. Contact, connection, respect, and love for other beings was their purpose.

"Good point, love," he murmured. "Many think that the inhabitants of these worlds are beneath them due to their lack of godly powers, when in truth, what would be the purpose of gods without these worlds to watch over? Without one, there is no other."

She rolled onto her stomach to look into Fenrir's eyes. "Exactly."

Chapter Nine

Hellion felt the shift in the stream when the Stone of Arthis was removed from its resting place. His remaining associates had taken a step back after the ogre attacks provided little results, and he was on his own, which suited him well.

Net and Fenrir were still out there searching for Forseti, and now they possessed a tool that could lead to the destruction of everything he'd built.

How and where had she found it?

Hellion had been searching for centuries and never once came across the stone. This changed everything. He would have to attend to this personally. The time for games had ended, and soon, so would their lives.

***

They woke to someone banging on their front door. Fenrir shifted into wolf and jumped off the bed to investigate. The sun hadn't even risen, and by the urgency of their pounding, he could already tell it was going to be a long day.

Fenrir commanded the door to open, revealing Agomon with his sword drawn. "Fenrir, the lands my people watch over are under attack. We need everyone's help to drive the beasts back."

Agomon came from a warrior race of gods who watched over a world inhabited by the Fae, a peaceful species unequipped to take on hordes of demons.

"I was led to believe the other gods were dealing with the attacks while we searched for Forseti." Had his fellow gods abandoned them?

"They are, but there's not enough to ensure the Fae aren't decimated," Agomon answered.

"We'll be right there," Net said as she joined them fully dressed in boots, jeans, and a black shirt while carrying both a gun and crossbow. If that weren't enough, she had a holster on her waist with grenades clipped to it.

"Where do you think you're going?" Fenrir asked. "It's too dangerous out there for you."

"Not with my shield, it's not. I want to help these people, and it sounds like they need all the help they can get. Set me up someplace high so that I can pick off as many as I can without getting in the way." She held up both weapons as if to stress her point.

"Where did you even get those?" Fenrir asked in confusion.

"From my amazing cupboard. The gun shoots cursed bullets to help slow the down the demons while the arrows are tipped with poison. A special blend with a predicted high efficacy rate. That ought to knock the wind out of them long enough for someone to behead the beasts. If not, I have these beauties for backup." Net shook her hips to emphasize the grenades.

"She's perfect, let's go," Agomon announced. "While we stand here and discuss this, Fae could be dying."

"I'll be safe," Net stated firmly. "It isn't as if I haven't battled before."

Fenrir took a deep breath and said, "You'd better be, or we will be having a discussion for centuries after this." She was right. They needed her help, and leaving her here unprotected was no better.

She smiled, set her hand on his fur, and they disappeared. Worst-case scenarios played out in his mind as they joined the stream heading straight for what sounded likely to be an even larger battle than the previous attacks. His mate was safe with her shield around her, but even then, it was a bitter pill for him to swallow.

"I will be fine, love." Her voice rang through their link. Over the last two days, their mating link had solidified, and now they could reach each other from anywhere. Their emotions and senses were aligned so much so that Fenrir could pick up Net's thoughts, as she could with his.

"I cannot help but worry about you." Fenrir tried to think of a way to explain his overwhelming need to keep her safe without coming off like an overbearing jerk.

"You don't need to explain. I, most of all, understand."

There was no truer statement. She'd endured so much for so long only to lose her powers. If anyone understood the need to keep safe and keep going, it was Net.

Fenrir slowed as they neared the battle to survey the area and find a place high enough for her to shoot from while remaining safe. A watchtower stood at the far end of the Fae community, and by the height of it, it would work well for this purpose.

With merely a thought, they stood on the sturdy boards of the tower. A thick metal railing encased the platform, and a ladder hung down from one side. He wanted to remove it so that no one could reach her, but then again, if she needed to get down and he couldn't get to her, removing the ladder would trap her.

"Go, my mate. They need you," she said as she lay down on her stomach against the rough wood, setting her weapons beside her. "Remember, I don't want to see a scratch on you."

Fenrir couldn't help but take a calming breath. She was a force to be reckoned with, and he simply had to get out of her way.

"Stay safe, mate," he said before disappearing and joining the battle below.

With one final look back, he saw her lining up her first shot with her rifle, and Fenrir ran into the fray.

***

The cold metal rested against her cheek as she searched for a beast. Demons were harder to spot in the dark. Their reptilian skin made them blend into their surroundings. While ogres stood out, there was nowhere for them to hide as big and ungainly as they were. Demons moved silently, holding dark and shadow to them. A movement to the right caught her eye, and she turned her gun in that direction in time to see a half-reptilian demon closing in on a young Fae who had yet to learn how to fly to safety.

Without hesitation, Net pulled the trigger, knocking the demon to the ground. A second Fae ran up to the creature and chopped off its head before taking the youngster away to safety.

She didn't have to look far for her next opportunity as an ogre ripped what she guessed was a thirty-foot tree from the ground and began using it to bat gods and Fae out of his way. Net switched to her enchanted crossbow with the poison-tipped arrows and began firing. The beauty of a magical crossbow. There was never a need to reload, the arrows simply appeared.

With each hit, the ogre slowed long enough for others to attack and bring it to the ground. Weapons varying from lightning bolts to swords broke the night's silence, causing a symphony of destruction. Several houses were burning, as well as a large building on the far side of the clearing.

Net wished she could bring the rain down to smother the flames, but her powers were in limbo, or at least she thought so until she felt the first drip land on her face. Sure enough, the sky opened up, and rain poured down. She wasn't sure she had caused the deluge, but welcomed it nonetheless. The sizzling sound of water hitting the flames was as satisfying as smoke plumes that replaced the fires.

For what felt like an eternity, but more realistically was thirty or forty minutes, Net shot round after round at the attackers before she began to notice their numbers were dwindling. For a brief moment, she allowed herself to hope until she felt a presence behind her.

In one fluid movement, she turned from her stomach onto her back and aimed at the man standing on the opposite side of the watchtower. Before she had a chance to take a shot, her weapon was hit by an unseen force sending it over the edge and out of reach. She jumped to her feet and raised her fists. Net wasn't going down without a fight.

The stranger hadn't said a word and kept his distance. She wasn't fooled. He was a grave threat. Her shield was glowing brighter than Net had ever seen before.

"What do you want?" she asked, the entire time attempting to reach Fenrir but receiving no reply. For a moment, she feared the worst, but quickly realized that he couldn't be dead, she would have known. Her heart would have shattered.

"You."

Well, wasn't that a creepy-ass reply. "Sorry, already spoken for."

"That dog? You might as well stop trying to reach him. I've blocked your connection." His smile looked more like a vicious slash across his face as his ebony eyes became ringed with red.

That statement made her push even harder to reach her mate. No one would keep him from her.

"Who are you?" She would have remembered him, with his dark robes and forked tongue.

"You may call me Hellion, your new god," he said before performing some grandiose bow the jerk had probably used countless times before.

"You can save the grand gestures. There's no one here to impress," she huffed. "What about me interests you?"

Hellion growled and took two steps to her closer, but Net's shield met him halfway, shocking him and forcing him back into the corner where he had first appeared.

"Tsk, tsk, tsk." Net waved her index finger at him. "See, now you've gone and ruined it. Just when we were getting to know each other."

"I will see you writhing in pain at my feet before you get anywhere near Forseti," Hellion raged.

"Ah, so you're the asshole responsible for all of this. Or perhaps a puppet for someone else. Your master, maybe?"

"I am no one's puppet." His eyes were no longer black, having turned entirely red.

She must have hit a button if the waves of anger pouring off him were anything to go by. Another important lesson: angry people do dumb things. Now was the time to see how far she could push.

"So, what's the grand plan? Take over existence and declare yourself king?" She'd been throwing that out there to see if he bit, but by the look on his face, she wasn't too far off the mark. "Seriously? You couldn't come up with anything more original? Well, isn't that embarrassing. I doubt you could've made it this far on your own."

She didn't miss his frequent glances at the ruby around her neck. Something about it worried the god. Good to know.

"They are nothing compared to my power. All shall bow before me—"

"Blah, blah, blah. Let me guess. They don't know you're breaking ranks, taking the lead, staging a coup. I'm sure they'll understand." This guy was too easy. Forseti may have taken her powers away, but her mind was as sharp as ever. Now she knew there was a group involved and that Hellion had declared himself all-powerful.

"I will rip you to pieces so that you resemble your brother," Hellion threatened while spit flew from his mouth.

"Ah, Vengier, ever the joy. You're the idiot who glued him back together." Net smiled and motioned to her chin. "You've got a little spittle right there."

Hellion used the sleeve of his cloak to wipe his face before saying, "It was simple for me to reanimate a creature so vengeful. His hate burns so brightly I could easily find a spark of life before he vanished."

"Yeah, I guess he'd be your kinda guy. But, for all your alleged power, you cannot touch me. Why do you think that is?" She batted her eyes and produced the sweetest smile, which had the desired effect of making him growl.

She was edging him closer to losing control, but she needed answers, and this asshole appeared to have them.

"You will not always have that shield to protect you. Once I've drained Forseti dry, I will have his power. Then I will come for you and make you pay for causing me so much trouble."

Net felt Fenrir's presence, and her tension evaporated. She may have a sharp tongue, and a barrier to protect her, but, ultimately, she was still powerless.

"Well, I see it's time for you to leave. I can assure you it hasn't been a pleasure," she stated seconds before a lightning bolt tore him from the tower and flung him far into the distance.

Fenrir appeared before her and took her into his arms. "Did he hurt you?"

"Nope. Hellion couldn't get past my shield." Thankfully.

"It didn't appear as though the two of you were making friends," he teased, and she noticed the sounds of battle had ceased.

Net looked around to find all the fighting was over. There wasn't a demon or ogre left standing. "Hellion and I don't see eye to eye regarding his belief he's to become king."

As she scanned the area, she didn't miss Agomon and a stunning Fae woman in each other's arms. The warrior god was brushing the dirt from her ebony hair as she stared at him adoringly. There was a story there, but that was for another time.

"King, interesting." Fenrir couldn't've rolled his eyes with more exaggeration.

"He is quite talkative when he's angry," Net said, not even trying to hide her smirk.

Fenrir's eyebrows shot up. "And I trust you were able to cause him to become angry, love."

Her smirk transformed into a wide smile. "Was there ever any doubt?"

"Not a one, mate," he stated with conviction.

***

"So, it's not one individual?" Meruim asked from across the kitchen table.

"Not according to Hellion," Net answered. It had been hours since the battle had ended and they returned to the cottage.

"He said he'd drain Forseti of his powers?" Thiesen asked what was beginning to feel like an interrogation. Or she could be cranky. She was hungry, tired, and in need of a shower.

"To use them to make himself king. Oh, and to make me pay for bothering him." That got a growl out of Fenrir. "Easy, big guy, I'm tougher than I look."

"Has anyone heard of this god Hellion before?" Abba asked as he joined them around the table. Net filled another mug with tea and handed it to him. Even though the gods didn't require sustenance, various commonplace niceties had been adopted by many.

"I've heard stories," Agomon stated. "However, I have no proof. Though a few of my fellow warrior gods recognized the creature on the watchtower with you."

Net leaned back into Fenrir's arms, her mortal body exhausted from the day's events. "Tell us what you know. Any information is better than what we currently have." Which wasn't much.

"Agreed," Fenrir stated. "I'd take conjecture and rumor over nothing."

Agomon set his mug down and sat a bit straighter on his chair. "It is said that he was responsible for his twin sister's death when they were toddlers. Questionable things would occur around him, animals went missing, the odd poisoning, random accidents, and more. The last straw came when his parents disappeared when Hellion was still a child, and he was sent away to a supervised facility."

"I'm guessing this wasn't like the boarding school I went to as a youth?" Net asked.

"Not in the least," Agomon stated. "Years passed and slowly, one by one, his minders grew ill until eventually, there was no one willing to deal with him. Forseti judged Hellion on his twenty-first birthday, and he was found guilty of a number of disturbing crimes. His sentence was much like your own, the loss of all his powers, but in his case, without the possibility of their return."

"Well, he certainly has them back now," Meruim stated while she continued to sharpen her dagger. Net was too tired to deal with her, and said nothing about the grating sound.

"No, not entirely," Agomon stated.

"Then how can he be immortal and so powerful?" Abba asked before turning to Meruim. "Seriously, now's the time to sharpen your blade?"

Net guessed he wasn't the only one annoyed by the incessant scraping.

"It comforts me and helps me think," Meruim replied without stopping. Abba shook his head in reply and looked away.

"Anyway, this is where the rumors come in," Agomon explained. "It is said among the Fae that one of their great leaders, Vruth, went missing only to reappear a year later. No longer the vibrant young man he used to be, but powerless, withered to skin and bone and babbling about a forest of souls and the return of Hellion."

Net was getting a sick feeling in the pit of her stomach. "Hellion did mention draining Forseti of his powers."

"We searched for this forest and came up with nothing. There wasn't a way to confirm Vruth's stories about trapped beings, chained to the ground of the forest."

That set off alarm bells. "In my nightmare, Forseti was chained to the ground, and I had to run through a forest to reach him."

"It would seem the rumors may be correct," Fenrir stated. "Is this Fae still alive?"

"I believe so," Agomon answered. "I will have to reach out to the current Fae leader to ask."

Net couldn't contain her yawn any longer, no matter how hard she tried. Her body felt heavy and awkward. Being mortal was exhausting.

"We will have to meet with him and see if he can tell us anything more about this place," Fenrir announced. "However, first, Net needs to rest."

Her head shot up, and she blinked her eyes to clear away the fog. "I'm fine. I don't want to slow us down. Not now that we're getting so close. We still haven't discussed my theory that the shield might protect us inside the forest."

"While I admire your spirit, Fenrir is right," Abba said. "You can barely keep your eyes open. You must rest."

Net knew they were right, but she was loath to admit it. "Fine, a few hours, that's all, and I'll be good as new."

One by one, the other four gods disappeared, and before she could say another word, Fenrir had her lying in bed naked and under thick covers.

"Rest now," he whispered into her ear, sending chills down her spine as he lifted her onto his chest.

"You're not playing fair," she grumbled while getting comfortable. His steady heartbeat was lulling her to sleep as he surely intended. "I'm strong enough to carry on."

"I'm sure I don't know what you mean." His chest bounced as he chuckled. "You're the strongest woman I know, love. Resting doesn't change that."

Her eyes shut before she could think of a comeback.

Chapter Ten

The home was straight out of a fairy tale. Flowered vines covered all four sides while a large willow tree loomed protectively over the thatched roof. The area was quiet and peaceful, and Net could hear water gurgling in a nearby stream.

The only thing that was out of place in this idyllic setting was the tall chain-link fence that surrounded the entire property. The first question that sprang to mind was, were they trying to keep people in or out?

The current leader of the Fae, Drummond, led the way to Vruth's home, and Net would be remiss if she hadn't noticed how far away it was from the Fae town.

"Does Vruth have many visitors?" she asked out of curiosity.

"Other than a select few Fae, no. He has requested it to be so," Drummond replied, and Net had to shield her eyes with her hand from the sun's rays reflecting off the leader's silver-blond hair. The Fae were peaceful and stunning people. Their inner beauty shone outwardly. They were stewards of the land, containing special magic unique to Fae. Net had always felt a kinship with them.

"How's he going to react to us showing up?" Fenrir asked. "Vruth knows we're coming, right?"

"He does. At first he was reluctant to see you. When I explained your mission and the information you're seeking, he agreed. But I must warn you, he isn't as he once was." Drummond's eyes were downcast for a moment before he continued. "You have to understand that he was once a strong, quick-minded leader."

"We've heard about his change in appearance when he returned." They already knew the story. Net couldn't imagine how heartbreaking those events must have been for Vruth and his family.

"It's more. Mentally he isn't what he used to be. He is easily confused and repeats words often. Most of the time, it's as if he doesn't realize others are in the room with him," Drummond explained.

Net understood that getting the information they needed wasn't going to be easy. But they had no choice if they wanted even the tiniest bit of detail about the forest and how to find it. Guilt sat heavily on her heart for having to put Vruth through this. Reliving those memories wouldn't be easy on him. But if he had any vestiges left of the leader he used to be, he'd want to help for the greater good.

As they neared the fence, an older woman came out of the front door of the home and met them at the gate. Her smile was warm but cautious.

"Good afternoon, Kayla. These are the gods that have come to speak with Vruth." Drummond waved his hand at the six of them.

"Hello to you all, but I must ask that only the woman wearing the ruby necklace enter," Kayla said, staring straight at Net. "The Divine Mother."

Instinctively, she reached up and held her hand over the pendant. How could Vruth have known that she had this? It wasn't exactly public knowledge. Perhaps he knew what she was supposed to do with it.

"I will not leave my mate's side," Fenrir rumbled from behind her, his deep growl reverberating through the space. No way she was willing to go in there alone and mortal.

Kayla's head cocked as if she were listening for something, but Net didn't hear a sound other than the birds perched among the tree branches. Maybe these people had the ability to communicate without speaking aloud.

"Vruth and Kayla are married," Drummond explained. "They have a bond that allows for personal communications."

"Am I that easy to read?"

"You wear your heart on your sleeve and emotions on your beautiful face, mate. That is one of the many reasons I love you. You do not hide away."

She hadn't realized that about herself, but if it were true, then Drummond's explanation made sense.

Learning the Fae had a bond similar to her and Fenrir's mating bond was exciting. It never ceased to amaze her that though their species appeared entirely different, there were still similarities between many of the beings of the realms and the gods. Which served to reconfirm her belief that they were all interconnected in some way as beings among these worlds were inevitably one.

"The wolf god is welcomed to enter as well," Kayla announced before unlatching the gate and opening it for them.

Net took a step forward and reached for Fenrir's hand before they followed Kayla down the winding stone path. Net noticed the care with which the plants and flowers were tended, from the smallest clover to the most abundant bloom. The knowledge somehow calmed her as they neared the front of the house.

Kayla turned to them as she opened the door and said, "Please come in." Her smile was warmer now than when they initially met. Net understood this had to be stressful for her to have six gods wanting to speak with her husband. The Fae may have lost their leader as he once was, but Kayla had lost her man, and the future they'd planned.

"Thank you for having us in your home," Net said as she laid her hand on Kayla's shoulder. "We understand how difficult this is for the both of you."

The older woman placed her hand on Net's forearm. "You will stop this creature you seek from harming any more souls."

Net wasn't sure if that was a statement or question but answered anyway. "Yes, we will."

Kayla nodded. "Thank you."

Once inside, she led them to a solarium located in the back of the house where they found Vruth sitting in an oversize chair waiting for them. His hair no longer shined like the other Fae, and his complexion didn't glow with health. His eyes were dimmed of light, and his body appeared to curl in on itself with his head bowed, arms tucked tight to his sides and legs pulled up to his chest.

Net's heart ached at what the poor man must have gone through. Fenrir squeezed her hand, and she continued forward.

"Would the two of you like to take a seat and I'll bring the tea out?" Kayla asked as she motioned to a nearby couch.

"Yes, thank you, Kayla," Fenrir replied.

For the next ten minutes, they sat in silence. Kayla had brought out the tea and served it to them before joining her husband, sitting in a chair by his side. Other than the initial introductions, not a word had been spoken. Net was unsure if she should ask questions or wait for Vruth to begin and was about to ask Fenrir through their link when the man looked up.

He sat cataloging every detail of their bodies both before speaking. "You seek Forseti?" His voice came out rough and cracked as if it were painful for him to speak.

"Yes."

He regarded her shrewdly. "To return your powers or to save a life?"

Net was taken back by the incisiveness of the question. "Both."

"What if it were a choice...choice?" he asked, and Net recalled Drummond mentioning the repeating of words. "One and not the other."

Net looked over at Fenrir. This conversation was going off the rails, and they hadn't even made it to the questions about the forest.

Fenrir spoke up. "Vruth, we are here to discuss the forest of souls. We believe that is where Hellion has trapped Forseti."

Vruth glanced over at Fenrir and said, "I know what you want," he said before turning to look at Net, clearly waiting for her reply.

Would she choose to have her powers back over saving a single life? Net thought about the crushing frustration and sadness she felt at the loss of something so vitally a part of who she was. The limitation and restrictions placed on her by Forseti's sentence had torn at her identity and self-worth. Even the thought of spending what was left of her mortal life like this, and perhaps worst of all, having limited time with her mate, made her stomach turn.

However, she went with the only answer her heart and conscience would allow. "To save a life."

Vruth's cloudy eyes seemed to be boring into her soul, but she didn't hide away. If the man wanted the truth, he'd already received it.

"The forest will kill all that enter," he began. "God or mortal alike."

"You made it out," Fenrir pointed out.

"Which had been his mistake... a mistake," he answered and began staring off into the distance. After a few moments, Kayla laid her hand on top of Vruth's, bringing him back from his memories.

"I'm sorry to make you relive this." Net could see the pain on his wrinkled face and shuddered at what he was remembering.

Vruth's brows furrowed, and he continued as if she'd said nothing. "Hellion received great satisfaction from sending me back... back to my wife in this condition. I will make him regret that decision."

Kayla wrapped her arms around her husband's shoulders. "I could not have gone on without you, dear. I blessed the day you returned to me."

Net could feel tears gathering in the corners of her eyes. This was not what she'd expected from coming here today. Fenrir's arm pulled her close, sensing her sadness.

"I will tell you the way to the forest," Vruth said. "But be warned, if you enter, you will never leave unless it suits Hellion's needs."

Net took in a deep breath and said, "Understood."

***

Fenrir as wolf paced around the cottage amid the usually tranquil sounds of the night, but tonight they were grating on his nerves. He dug his sharp claws into the earth with every step as he tried to keep his raging emotions in check so as not to wake Net. He didn't fail to notice the worn path he was creating with his pacing.

They were to leave in the morning for the forest of souls, and with every minute that passed his anxiety ballooned. Vruth's warnings echoed in his head on repeat, and Fenrir's desire to take Net far away from all of this grew stronger by the minute.

This could not be happening all over again. His mate was putting herself in danger, and he could do nothing about it. Old pain and anger rose until he felt as if he were choking on it. As a god, he knew the Fates could be cruel, but this was a new low for even them.

"So, what lap are you on?" Meruim's voice jarred him out of his thoughts to find the goddess sitting on a nearby stump. "Going for some kind of record?"

"This isn't a good time for your shit, Meruim," Fenrir growled. "Leave me be."

"Leave you to fester is more like it. I'd love to, but if we're going to attempt this rescue in the next few hours, we need everyone's head in the game."

Fenrir stopped and growled. "You're one to talk. Since the beginning of this mission, you've been a thorn in everyone's side. Save me the lecture."

"Touché." She laughed. "However, Net has that shield and the skill to take care of herself. When you get past all the girly, flowery bullshit, you'll find a woman who could kick my ass." Meruim's voice grew deeper, more menacing. "Don't ever tell her I said that or I would be forced to hunt you down."

He huffed out his frustration and finally sat. "Without her powers, she's vulnerable. I refuse to lose her."

"So, you hide out and wait for Hellion to come to you. If he does what he says he's going to do, it's only a matter of time before that happens," Meruim explained.

"Since when have you looked at things logically? Aren't you the one who fights first and asks questions later?" That had been her reputation, and for good reason. As he'd witnessed, it was true.

"You give the people exactly what they expect, and then they don't ask any questions."

Fenrir stopped his racing mind and looked at Meruim. "Is that what you've been doing?"

"This isn't about me," she said. "You have to allow Net to make her own choices. She knows the stakes better than all of us. You can't stop her from doing the right thing."

"Perhaps I've misjudged you, Meruim."

She pulled out her dagger and said, "No, you haven't," before disappearing into the night.

Meruim was a walking contradiction, leaving Fenrir wondering which version of the goddess was real.

Chapter Eleven

Considering Vruth's directions were in reverse since he was leaving the forest on his way back to Fae lands, they would take their time ensuring they didn't miss any of the markers Vruth had left behind.

Agomon was still furious to learn the forest Hellion had been using to drain people of their lives and powers had been on one of the planets the warrior gods watched over. No matter how they each tried to explain to him that if Hellion were able to hide Forseti's location, a forest would be easy enough for him to make disappear. Net doubted Agomon would ever forgive himself for his perceived failure.

Vruth had explained that he'd been silent on the location until now, not wanting to lead anyone to their deaths. Net was still undecided if that was a positive sign of his confidence in them.

"Okay, once we make it to the first marker, those intent on stopping us will know we are on the move," Fenrir stated, looking more nervous than Net had ever seen him.

"It won't be long before we have visitors. The Fae may have been able to hide our presence while speaking with Vruth, but that help ended at the border of their lands," Agomon stated.

Net was getting the distinct impression that the five of them were directing these instructions to her. She was mortal, not an imbecile.

Meruim even decided to chime in. "We'll need to find the marker as quickly as possible to determine our next direction."

Net had enough of whatever they were playing at. "Why the hell are you all staring at me when you say those things? It's not as if I don't know the plan already. I helped create it. Are you afraid that I'll mess this up?" That thought hurt. She'd been holding her own since the beginning, god-like powers or not.

"It's not that we're afraid of you screwing up, it's that you are the most important person in this plan. Forseti chose you, and you have the ruby that he'd wanted to be found. Without you, this whole thing goes up in smoke," Fenrir explained.

"Guys, let's not heap that pressure on until she freaks out," Thiesen said. "She's got this."

"Thank you, Thiesen."

"I'm sorry, mate," Fenrir said as he gathered her into his arms. "You are everything to me, and I'm having a hard time accepting the danger you will be in. I chose to fixate on the plan instead of telling you how I felt."

Net hugged him tightly. "I understand. I will move as quickly as possible while you five keep a lookout for our welcoming party. Remember, I have my shield, so take care of yourselves. We will make it to the forest and free Forseti."

Fenrir nodded his head, but Net knew nothing she could say would calm him until this mission was over.

"It's time to get this show on the road," Meruim snarled, pulling two swords from the sheaths on her back. "There are a few gods that need a reckoning."

Net smiled at the fierce woman, shocking herself. Was she beginning to like Meruim? That couldn't be right.

"Ready?" Fenrir asked her while kissing Net's temple.

Net held her hand over the ruby hanging around her neck. She had memorized each description of where to find the location markers Vruth had given them. She wanted all this to be over so that she and Fenrir could start their mated life together.

"Hell yes."

When they arrived at the first location outside of Fae lands, they found it quiet. The other four spread out among the trees while Fenrir stayed by her side. They were looking for a tree with a twisted trunk and red flowers growing around its base. Net looked in all directions.

"There are red flowers under all these trees. They must have spread over the years. We have to find the twisted trunk." Net began systematically walking through the rows of trees surrounded by red flowers.

Precious time was being wasted, but she couldn't blame Vruth for that, it had been many years since he'd been in this spot. She was about ready to backtrack when Fenrir called her.

"Net, is this it?" he asked.

She ran to his side, and sure enough, he'd found the twisted tree. Net went to her knees, looking for the stone Vruth had left. The old Fae had enough power to leave a memory of his journey behind. The stones he'd hidden would give her a visual image and direction to the next location once she held it in her palm.

In a small knot at the base of the tree, Net found the stone and pulled it free. She held it in the palm of her hand, and the image appeared in her mind. Once she relayed the information to Fenrir, they were ready to go, and not a moment too soon.

Explosions lit up the area as debris rained down. Fenrir shifted into wolf, and Net climbed onto his back before disappearing.

They reached the second location with the other gods by their side. Net had worried that one might be left behind still fighting, but all were safe, for now.

"They're on to us now, we need to move faster," Abba said before disappearing into the mist coming in from the coast.

Net scanned the cliff, looking for the stone she prayed hadn't weathered away over the years. Luckily, she found it easily. The stone in the shape of a dagger sat underneath a rocky overhang, protecting it from the elements.

"There," Net said from her perch on Fenrir's back while pointing in the direction she wanted him to go. "Under the rocks."

Fenrir ran toward the stone moments before Vengier appeared before them. "Sister, here you are. I've been looking everywhere for you."

"Sorry, not in the mood for a reunion right now," Net snapped. Desperately trying not to gag at the smell coming from him. "I'm guessing Hellion hasn't found you useful enough to bother returning you to whole."

Net slid from Fenrir's back to stand, readying for the moment Vengier attacked. Fenrir would deal with him while she went for the rock.

"You're in no shape to fight me, Vengier," Fenrir stated. "Why don't you—"

Whatever her mate was about to say was cut off by her brother's angry scream. "You mated another dog."

She brought her hand up to rub her fingers over the scar from her mating bite. "Sure did."

Her mate growled deep before saying, "Net is my mate, and you will not touch her."

Vengier's eyes bulged from his head, and his body shook with anger. In his condition, Net expected pieces to start falling off, but he held it together, physically, not mentally. His crazy was on full display.

"Decisions, decisions. I've already gotten rid of both of your first mates, so which of you should I make single once again?" Vengier taunted.

Fenrir didn't give him time to decide and attacked Vengier head-on. Net took off running for Vruth's stone when Phume appeared in her path and attempted to reach for her. The moment Phume's hands touched Net's shield, the goddess screamed in pain, pulling her hands back to find flesh hanging from the bones of her fingers.

Net had no idea her shield could inflict that much damage. She'd assumed the shield was for defense alone. With a flick of her arm, she lashed her shield out like a whip, catching Phume across the knees and taking her to the ground.

Even though she deserved to be judged, Net wasn't the one to do that, and she would not have Phume's demise on her hands. It was another thing entirely if she were forced to fight to the death, but Phume wasn't in any shape to attack again, so Net went for the rock. Similar to before, the moment she touched the cold surface, an image appeared to her with directions, which she relayed to Fenrir.

She looked up in time to see Vengier running away before disappearing altogether. Phume was long gone as well, and Net wondered if the goddess would be able to heal her wounds. Whatever power in this shield Forseti had given her was, it certainly proved more potent than she'd given it credit for.

To confirm she had control of her shield, Net threw out her arm, and a whip appeared once again. "Cool."

"New toy, mate?" Fenrir asked as he neared. "Nice job with Phume. I don't think she'll forget that encounter any time soon."

"It would seem I haven't been using my shield to its full potential." She could have been of more use in battle.

"I must say this does alleviate a bit of my worry. Ready to go?" Fenrir asked.

"Yes, the sooner we find Forseti, the sooner you and I can go home."

"Sweeter words have never been spoken, mate," Fenrir said before Net climbed back on his back, and they headed to the next location.

The process repeated itself several times over, with a different mixture of demons, gods, and ogres showing up shortly after they'd arrive at a location. Now that Net could put on some sort of offense, she took full advantage of her shield. She was letting it flow around her at command, even once wrapping her shield around Fenrir when an ogre almost fell over top of him.

Meruim, Agomon, Thiesen, and Abba kept most of the attacks at bay, but a few demons managed to get past them, and that's where Fenrir stepped in along with her. Net wouldn't deny the joy she was feeling at being able to do her part during each skirmish.

Fighting side by side with her mate gave her a sense of purpose she'd been missing since her sentence. With each clue, they were getting closer to their goal, and she allowed hope to creep in. They would free Forseti, and everything would go back to the way it was, including her powers. Then she'd spend her time protecting all beings from gods bent on subjugating them. Recent events had opened her eyes.

She'd come a long way from being the goddess trapped in a dying forest, and she had no intention of ever turning back.

***

Fenrir watched his mate in awe. The speed at which she mastered the various weapons of her shield was impressive. One moment she used her whip to force demons back while producing a sword-like shape from her shield to attack.

However, he had also noticed the feeling of malice growing stronger with each stone they found, and the earth became parched as if all life had been drained away. Fenrir was sure Hellion was responsible for this, along with his forest of souls he'd created.

Not a single bird or ground animal could be seen, and if Fenrir's calculations were correct, they were one clue away from their destination. When they appeared at the last location, gone were any previous bits of vegetation. Rocks and sand surrounded them, which posed a problem for finding the last marker.

"Any idea where we start looking?" Meruim asked, waving at the stone-covered land.

When Net didn't respond, Fenrir turned to find her kneeling on the ground. Concerned, he joined her to see what she'd found. When he did, Fenrir shifted and lifted his mate into his arms. It was chilling to realize that the white specks on the ground were bones, some complete skeletons partially buried in sand while others were in pieces.

The rest of the team stood silent vigil over the makeshift graveyard. No one was certain of what to say or even think. The bones went on for as far as the eye could see, and he was having a hard time wrapping his mind around the fact that each represented a being whose life had been cut short by a madman.

Agomon reached down and plucked a silver button from the ground. "All this was under our noses all this time, and we didn't see it." His voice was rough with emotion, and Fenrir could hear the disgust in his voice. "How can I ever call myself a guardian of the Fae again? I don't deserve such a title after such a monumental failure."

Meruim walked over to him and took the button from his shaking hand before having a closer look. Fenrir noticed many more buttons scattered on the ground made of the same silver as the first.

Pain, sharp and deadly, followed by anger swept through all of them before Meruim managed to get her emotions under control. She placed the button in the pocket of her jeans, turned, and walked several feet away.

Theisen picked up another button and examined the engraving moments before his mouth fell open in shock.

"What is it?" Net asked from the safety of Fenrir's arms.

"The button has a particular engraving," Theisen began before handing the button to Fenrir as if unwilling to say more.

He took a look and instantly knew whose insignia this was. Meruim's. "How long has your army been missing, Meruim?"

"Close to a year." Her voice was distant as if lost in thought.

"And you've been searching ever since?" Abba asked.

"Yes," she replied without turning around. "I was to join them for a celebration, but when I arrived, they'd all disappeared. They were good soldiers, every one of them, with families still waiting for their return."

"Hellion took them," Net gasped. "I'm so sorry, Meruim."

Meruim's back straightened. "Hellion is mine."

"If I have the opportunity to save him for you, I will, but if I have the chance, I will take it." Fenrir wanted to be clear. If it were a choice of ending Hellion's reign of fear or risking his escape so that Meruim could have her revenge, he'd bring Hellion to his end.

"Understood."

"First, we need to find that stone," Theisen interjected while raising his hands in mock defeat. "There are millions of them."

Net gestured for Fenrir to put her down, which he did, and she walked over to what looked like the charred remains of a tree trunk and plucked a stone from inside the burnt-out husk.

"This is the last stone. The forest of souls will be next," Net said as she transferred the image to Fenrir. "Are we ready for this?"

"As ready as I'll ever be," Thiesen groaned and stretched out his back as if it were stiff. As a god, that was impossible. "All this fighting is taking its toll on me."

Honestly, what could he expect from a god accustomed to leisure?

Net walked back over to Fenrir and melted back into his arms, exactly where he wanted her.

"Does anyone else wonder why no one has come to attack us here?" Agomon asked as he scanned the horizon. "They've attacked at every other location before this."

True and not unexpected. A tactical decision to have no one try to stop them from going any farther.

"They're waiting for us outside the forest," Net said as she faced them all. "There's no other explanation."

"We will face them there and make them pay for what they've done." Meruim was primed for battle. Her determination clear for all to see. "We'll bring the fight to them."

"Should we call in reinforcements?" Theisen asked, not looking nearly as fierce as Meruim or as confident.

"Already done," Fenrir assured before shifting into his wolf. "Stay close to me, Net."

His mate climbed onto his back and laid her head on the thick fur around his neck before squeezing tight. "There is no other place I'd rather be."

Chapter Twelve

Net would be lying if she said she hadn't considered for a split second calling the whole thing off. She'd begun to care for these people, and even now, she might be leading them to their deaths.

"You are not responsible for anyone's actions other than your own." Fenrir's voice reached out to her through their link. *"Each one has made their choice, and no one is forcing them into battle. They believe in this and you, my love."*

Before she could answer, they arrived at the last location, and sure enough, they had a welcoming party. With their backs to the forest, the six faced legions of ogres and demons. Vengier and Phume were among the handful of gods in attendance. Since the last defeat in battle, it seemed Hellion's god-following numbers had diminished.

Net didn't have long to wonder where Hellion was, as he appeared in a flourish of smoke and lightning. Seriously, how overinflated was this god's ego?

"I see you didn't heed my warnings to stay away. Now it comes to this. You will die here along with the thousands before you." Hellion spoke of death with little regard and evident glee.

"Think so?" Meruim growled. "I'll be flaying the flesh from your bones before this night is through."

Net took the opportunity to glance over at Phume, surprised to see bandages on her hands. Phume hadn't been able to heal the wounds caused by Net's shield. It was time to test a theory.

It hadn't taken as much concentration to surround their group with her shield, but she wanted to see what happened when she pushed it outward. On her command, the shield snaked out toward their enemies, and every time it neared a god, they quickly vanished out of its way.

Unfortunately, the same couldn't be said for the ogres and demons, who were simply pushed back by the shield without major injury.

Good to know.

"It would appear the gods can't protect themselves from the shield causing them injuries, but the others are simply unable to breach the shield walls," Fenrir spoke through their link but shared the knowledge with their team as well.

"You believe yourself to be powerful, Net, but you are nothing to Forseti. You're a means to an end. As soon as you free him, you'll go back to your sentence, no powers, no protection." Hellion's voice was beginning to grate on her last nerve.

"Are we here to talk or fight?" Meruim asked, clearly eager for the battle to begin.

"How typical, the same goddess itching for bloodshed every chance she gets," Hellion growled.

"Only if it's your blood we're talking about," Meruim countered.

"What a shame. You could have been useful to our cause. Your lust for blood rivals my own."

"Never would've happened," she remarked. "I'm allergic to egomaniacs and idiots."

Net noticed Hellion's eyes flare red as they had done when he'd appeared on the watchtower. Meruim was as successful at pissing the asshole off as she was. Go, girl.

Meruim looked over at her and winked. Had she heard Net's thoughts? That would be impossible unless… "Fenrir, is our link still open to the team?"

"Yes," Meruim answered before her mate could. "You want a turn at Hellion? I'm willing to share."

Net couldn't help but laugh, angering the would-be king even more. "This is your last chance to swear allegiance to me or die where you stand," Hellion bellowed, pacing outside the edge of her shield.

"That's your sales pitch?" Abba chuckled. "No wonder there are so few gods with you."

"Good one," Meruim chuckled, but never once took her glare off Hellion.

"Kill them," Hellion ordered, and his legions moved forward. Of course, the gods remained back, preferring to send their minions as fodder.

Net felt their presence before they arrived. Gods and goddesses began appearing in the clearing one after the other, and for the first time, Net saw fear on Hellion's face. It looked good on him, and she'd endeavor to keep it there.

As the new arrivals attacked, Net kept her shield around their team. "We have to go into the forest and find Forseti. There's no other choice."

"Wait a minute. I was under the impression whoever enters the forest dies." Theisen looked ready to bolt. "Slowly and painfully."

"You only die if you can't get out, or if you run into a Writhen," Net explained. "I, for one, intend to get out and take down any Writhen that gets in my way."

"Great, after everything I've been through, I'm going to die," Theisen grumbled.

Net began backing toward the forest of souls. "If you wish to remain here, then I understand. However, we are going into the forest."

Thiesen edged back, staying within the confines of the shield. At any time, the god could simply disappear and take himself far away from here. But he didn't.

The team continued toward the forest as the battle played out in front of them. As they moved closer to the edge of the trees, Hellion appeared before them, careful to stay outside her shield's reach.

"If it is my forest you seek, by all means, enter so that I may drain the life from you all and use it against those you hold dear." Hellion's smile was cruel, promising to carry out what he'd threatened.

Net had had enough of this asshole. She raised her hand and brought out her whip before Hellion had a chance to teleport away, catching him across his neck. His scream of rage was the last thing they heard before they passed the outer limits of the forest.

Once inside its boundaries, the world beyond seemed to disappear. No longer could they hear the sounds of battle or Hellion's taunting words. It felt as if they were in a bubble of silence, forcing Net to speak aloud to make sure she could still be heard.

"Everyone okay?"

She watched as each god checked themselves over to confirm there wasn't any drain on their powers. Net held tight to Fenrir, unwilling to release him out of fear he would be harmed if she did. They knew little about the forest's capabilities, which worried her most of all. You couldn't have prepared fully when you didn't know what was coming for you.

"It would appear your shield is protecting us from the effects of the forest. We must be sure to stay under it while we search," Fenrir stated, "or we'll be open to attack."

"Thank goodness," Net said as she slid from her mate's back. "That's what I was hoping would happen once we got in here."

"Hoping? You didn't know?" Meruim asked incredulously.

"Let's say I was going on that assumption and had high confidence it would work," Net explained.

Meruim threw her hands into the air. "Thanks for letting us know."

"I did try to start the conversation in the meeting that you couldn't stop yourself from sharpening those daggers the entire time. Would it have changed your decision either way?"

"No," Meruim growled.

"Then why are we arguing?" Net asked. Her nerves were shot, and adding any additional stress was not a good idea.

"I don't know," Meruim yelled back.

Net burst out laughing at the absurdity of this moment. They'd found all the clues and fought numerous battles along the way. Faced off with legions of beasts commanded by a madman and survived various attempts on their lives. Now, they stood on the precipice of completing their mission, in a forest that drained the life from its victims, and they were arguing over who knew what when. There was really no other choice but to laugh for her own sanity.

Slowly, Meruim's anger dissipated until she too began laughing along with Net.

"I think they've finally snapped," Abba said aloud. "What should we do?"

"No, I think they've finally found common ground," Fenrir explained. "Stress can bring people together as well as tear them apart."

Net didn't know who was right, but she hoped it was Fenrir because now would be the wrong time to lose her sanity. Their laughter slowed, and Net wiped the tears from her eyes. She'd needed that. The laughter was cathartic after what felt like years of worry.

"Let's get this rescue party moving," Agomon stated as he continued to scan the forest around them. "Which way do we go from here?"

Net scanned the area. It reminded her of the forest from her nightmares. Towering trees stood like sentinels while their branches reached out and intertwined with the other spindly branches beside it. What seemed like walls of limbs reminded her of the struggle she had weaving through them to get to Forseti.

"This is straight out of my nightmares. Keep your eyes out for a Writhen. It tended to show whenever I got close to Forseti," Net told them as she felt the cold seep in from their surroundings. Typically, the Divine Mother was at home in all forests, but this one was not a part of the natural world, and held nothing of Net's influence. This fabrication was created by pure evil and behaved in the same manner.

She had noted a particular tree from her nightmares that she'd repeatedly come across because of its resemblance to an actual person. Holes in the trunk were placed to resemble eyes and a gaping mouth. Two large branches stretched out from its sides as if reaching for her, while its large roots snaked in and out of the ground around it.

"I recognize that tree," Net said as she pointed at where it stood.

"Great, the creepy one," Theisen grumbled. "Why is it always the creepy one?"

"Everything is creepy about this place," Abba said while still holding his flaming sword at the ready. Much like the rest of the team with their weapons. "It's as good a place to start as any."

"Can everyone stop using the word creepy? We know it is, we have yes," Meruim snapped.

Net sunk her fingers into Fenrir's thick coat and began walking forward, making sure that the shield held and surrounded them all. The ground cracked under their feet like eggshells with every step, filling the air with a continual crunching noise. No forest animals appeared as the gods made their way through the undergrowth. Net hadn't expected to see any life in this place. This forest was dead even though there were leaves still on the trees and the sun in the sky.

When they neared the tree, the ruby pendant around her neck began to warm against her skin.

Sensing the change, Fenrir stopped and looked at her. "Are you well, mate?"

Net held the ruby away from her skin to have a better look at it, and if she wasn't mistaken, the jewel appeared to be glowing. "It's heating up the closer we get to the tree."

"And glowing," Meruim added.

"Is it hurting you?" Fenrir asked, ever the protector.

Net thought about it before answering, making sure there wasn't an effect on her body that she was missing. "No, the change startled me, but it's not painful."

"Promise me that you'll remove it if that changes," Fenrir stated. "In any way."

Net couldn't help but smile. "I promise."

They took a single step closer to the tree, and the ground began to shake. The tree appeared to sway as the dry soil rolled beneath it. The branches twisted and turned in a sort of bizarre dance.

"Now what?" Abba growled while turning in circles, trying to find the threat.

The "face" on the tree was becoming more lifelike by the second. This couldn't be good. A yellow glow began to emanate from somewhere inside the tree's trunk, and its roots were not only snaking through the soil, but lifting straight out of it.

"Tell me that everyone else is seeing this tree come to life," Thiesen demanded. "I'm not losing it, right? I have been under a lot more stress than is healthy."

"No, it's not you. However, I think we should back up," Net suggested with nervous laughter seconds before those branches thrust forward, reaching out for them.

"Back up out of its reach," Fenrir ordered while placing himself in front of Net, but it was too late. The roots behind them were already cutting off their retreat.

More roots from under their feet sprang up to surround them, and her shield wasn't keeping them out. Each of them began hacking at the thick roots, but it wasn't slowing them down. As quickly as they chopped off one, another root rose to take its place.

"Why is the shield not working?" Agomon yelled while waving his sword back and forth, chopping off anything that got close enough. He was a magnificent warrior.

"I don't know." Net threw her arm out, requesting her whip, and used it to begin slicing through their subterranean attackers as well. "The whip still works as a weapon, but the shield isn't keeping them out. My best guess is that the forest is supposed to be a part of nature, not an evil being." Forseti couldn't be expected to think of every possibility while being held captive here.

"Another one of Hellion's surprises," Thiesen yelled to be heard over the sound of the cracking earth and the clash of swords against roots as thick as a man's arm.

Fenrir raked his sharp claws along the length of root headed straight for Net, stopping it in its tracks. This carried on for several more minutes, and she was starting to worry the roots would never stop coming at them when one surfaced directly beneath her. Within seconds, it wrapped itself around her and lifted her high into the air as it tightened its hold.

"Net," Fenrir hollered, getting the attention of the other four.

He bit and slashed at the root, trying to make it release her, but it continued to wind its way around her, drawing ever closer to her face. Meruim joined Fenrir, using her swords to stab at it, as well as Thiesen, while the other two kept the remaining roots at bay.

It was becoming difficult for her to take a deep breath as she struggled against the building pressure. Net tried to pull one of her arms free, but it wouldn't budge.

"Hold on, mate. We'll get you free."

She was desperately trying to remain conscious as the sounds of her ribs breaking filled her senses. If she passed out, she wouldn't be able to hold the shield around the others, leaving them vulnerable to Hellion's drain on their powers. After the first initial wave of pain, Net felt nothing. However, her eyesight was getting dimmer around the edges, no matter how hard she fought.

For a moment, she thought all was lost as the roots worked their way up her rib cage. However, as it continued to wind its way around her chest, it brushed against the ruby pendant. A hideous screeching noise filled the air as the root burst into ash, releasing her in midair.

Fenrir broke her fall when he caught her in his arms on her way down. Gently, he lowered her the rest of the way down while checking her for injuries.

"Where does it hurt?" he asked, skipping over the pretense that she wasn't injured. She figured he knew getting a bear hug from a cursed tree root was bound to leave a mark.

"My ribs. I think it broke a few." She'd felt them crush as it was squeezing her. One thing she'd learned from her sentence: being mortal was painful.

Fenrir laid her on the ground while the others formed a circle around them, watching for any new threats. They'd come a long way as a team. From squabbling children to cohesive unit, Net couldn't have been prouder.

"This will help, my love," Fenrir said before placing his hands over her rib cage.

"Being mortal sucks," she growled out her pain and frustration. "I can't wait to have my immortality and powers back."

A warmth filled her as his hands began to glow brighter. It was an odd feeling having her bones knit back together, not exactly painful, but not altogether right. Soon she was able to take a deep breath and was thankful for it.

"So much better," Net said between breaths. "Thank you, mate."

Fenrir helped her stand, and it was the first chance she had to survey the damage. Piles of ash covered the torn-up area, and there wasn't a root left in sight. When she looked over at where the tree trunk had been, there was nothing left but a large pile of ash being dispersed by the breeze.

"What the hell just happened?" Meruim asked, kicking her boot through a nearby pile. "One minute, we're losing the battle, and the next, everything stops."

"The root touched my pendant," Net said while holding the ruby away from her skin. "And this happened." Waving her hands around the area in question.

"The ruby killed it?" Abba asked.

"That's the best answer I have." Net shrugged her shoulders. "There's no other way to explain it."

"What else can happen?" Thiesen groaned. "Watch, there'll be more than a single Writhen in these woods."

"You had to curse us," Meruim snarled, "didn't you?"

"Shit."

Chapter Thirteen

Hellion batted another lightning strike away as he drew his sword. Fenrir, Net, and their band of miscreants made their way into his forest, but he, as of yet, was unable to draw power from them. The effect should have been instantaneous, and though he'd been looking forward to battling them, draining their lives slowly would do quite nicely. He could make them last for decades, barely alive, chained to the ground.

He wasn't surprised when half of those vying for positions among their newly formed council vanished at the sight of the other gods coming to help rescue Forseti. Weak, each one of them. He would remember all those who'd betrayed the cause, and when he was crowned king, they'd never have the chance to do it twice.

His ogres flooded the battlefield, slowing the invaders while demons stayed to the outskirts, searching for openings to attack while their foes were distracted. Of course, ogres and demons were no match for a god, but if his forces delivered enough damage, most would be forced to leave and regroup, giving him more time with the victims in his forest.

Soon he would have enough power to rule them all. Hellion would re-create the worlds in his image of perfection, starting with those shifters.

***

Fenrir couldn't slow his racing heart no matter what he tried. Seeing Net wrapped in roots had been terrifying. He had failed to protect her, and she'd been hurt. He'd never wanted her to regain her immortality more than he did right now. She'd be safer, and his mistakes wouldn't risk her life.

"Enough, mate. You are not responsible for my being hurt, Hellion is. You, my love, are responsible for taking the pain away

and healing me." Net's voice rang through their link along with love.

"I should have been able to keep the roots away from you," Fenrir argued.

"There were dozens of them coming out everywhere. No one could have caught all of them," Net countered.

Though logically he knew she was right, his anger at himself wasn't going anywhere anytime soon.

"Thank you, mate. I will try to see it your way."

"Yeah, like I believe that." She laughed, improving his mood substantially. *"You are not responsible for other people's actions."*

"Using my own words against me now."

"If I have to." Net dug her fingers deeper into his fur on the back of his neck. *"I will."*

He loved his mate for many reasons, her compassion being one of them.

"I think I recognize that stand of trees over there," Net said aloud while pointing off to the right. "It reminds me of the ones I had to squeeze my way through to find Forseti on the other side."

The six of them stopped a few feet away from the thick tree trunks that formed what appeared to be a solid wall.

"Do you remember how you made it past this, mate?" Fenrir asked while surveying the area.

Net took a step closer, trying to bring up the memory of how she made it through to the other side. She remembered being low to the ground and something about the branches. Kneeling down, Net realized what she had done before.

"We have to crawl through, low to the ground where the branches thin out." The others bent to have a look when she remembered another critical fact. "On the other side of this was where I found the Writhen."

"Why am I not surprised," Thiesen groaned, and Net was beginning to feel sorry for him. It wasn't as if he'd been a warrior god before Forseti went missing. All this had to be overwhelming for a god used to leisure.

"I should lead the way," Net suggested, considering she'd done it before. "It's coming back to me now."

"How about someone else goes through first?" Fenrir asked. "The safest place for you is between the five of us so that we can protect you."

"I have my shield," she reminded him.

"Yes, but it didn't stop the roots." Fenrir shifted to man and cupped the side of her face. "Please, do this for me. I don't know how much more I can take of you being in danger."

Net had felt his terror when that root had attacked her and understood his concerns. "Okay, I'll follow the first one in to help with navigating through the branches."

Fenrir smiled and seemed relieved. "Thank you."

"I'll go first," Meruim said. "If there is a Writhen waiting for us, I'll be ready for him."

"Agreed. I'll follow behind Net," Fenrir said before shifting back to wolf.

Net searched for the perfect spot for Meruim to enter and then followed her in. The branches tore at her exactly as she remembered, and the rough bark scratched her skin, but she never once stopped. Forseti was close. She could feel it.

Light began to filter in through the branches as they neared the opposite side of the tree wall, and Net prepared herself for whatever would be waiting for them. Meruim broke through the last of the limbs and stood. Net quickly followed and was shocked by what she found.

Writhens, plural. There had to be a dozen of the beasts milling around Forseti's chained form, waiting for the gods to try to free him. On each of their grotesque heads, their six beady eyes turned at once in the direction of the gods. The element of surprise was lost on a Writhen, considering each eye could move independently of one another.

Fenrir came through, placed himself between them and Net. Once the last two gods had crawled through, it was decision time.

"Options?" Net asked.

"We rush them and take them out," Meruim said.

"Any other options?" Net asked, shaking her head at her friend. Friend? Was Meruim her friend? Obviously, now wasn't the time to have a shopping trip to the mall to find out how close they'd become, but Net smiled wryly at the thought.

"The way I see it, we have to get Net to Forseti," Agomon said. "She's the one Forseti reached out to in order to save him."

"Anybody else wondering why the beasts aren't charging us already?" Abba asked.

"Be thankful they're not." Meruim pulled out one of her daggers. "Here, just in case."

Net took it and held it at the ready. "Thank you, my friend." The sentiment caused Meruim to smile briefly.

"What about the shield?" Thiesen asked. "How far can we spread out before we're vulnerable?"

"I'm not sure, we never tested it, but I'll do my best to hold it as long as I can." That was the only guarantee she could give.

"I will take you as close as we can get to Forseti," Fenrir said. "If I get taken down, you keep going while I fight them off. The most important thing is freeing Forseti."

"I will not risk you," Net said as she looked around. "Any of you. You're important as well."

The others glanced at each other before Fenrir continued. "If it comes down to a choice between us and freeing Forseti, you must choose The Judge. He is the only one who can set things right again."

Net wrapped her arms around Fenrir's neck and hugged him close. "Don't make me have to choose. Stay safe. All of you."

She climbed back onto Fenrir's back and held on tight to his thick ruff. They would race forward as a unit, and if one slowed or engaged a beast, she'd try to maintain a shield around them for as long as she could.

"Ready?" Fenrir asked.

Net sucked in a lungful of air and said, "Go."

The tension doubled as the Writhens moved forward as a unit, sensing the gods were on the move. Fenrir dug his claws into the dry ground seconds before he took off straight for Forseti. The Writhens began charging the shield using the long spikes on their backs as battering rams, causing breaks to form on the surface of Net's shield.

The beasts were left over from the dawn of these planets. No one knew how far their magic could go. The spikes began glowing red as they continued to hammer at the shield, forcing Net to concentrate harder than she ever had before to make it hold.

The other four gods were still inside the protection of the shield, but it wasn't going to last a lot longer. She not only had to worry about the beasts, but if her shield failed, they'd be vulnerable to Hellion's forest of souls.

They were only a few hundred yards from Forseti and closing fast. There was a Writhen above them using its jagged beak to punch a hole through the top.

"It's not going to hold much longer," Net yelled. "Be ready."

No sooner had she spoken the words then the shield shattered and disappeared altogether. Net could feel the draw on her strength almost immediately. The forest would continue doing so until they were dead if the Writhens did do the job first.

Meruim and Abba fought back to back as Agomon and Thiesen flanked her and Fenrir. A Writhen was barreling straight for them, nostrils flared, sickle-shaped claws open wide, and at the last second, they changed directions, leaving the beast to slam into a nearby tree.

As they approached the spot where Forseti was chained to the ground, Fenrir said, "Jump off, and we will surround you while you free Forseti."

"Have we figured out how to do that yet?" Agomon asked.

"No."

"Shit."

The moment Fenrir stopped, Net leapt from his back, expending a lot more energy than she'd felt before. The forest was beginning to affect her, and by the slower movements of the other gods, they were feeling it too.

She slid to a stop in front of Forseti, who appeared to be unconscious. Net used the dagger Meruim had given her to chip away at the chains, but even though she was using an enchanted blade, Net was getting nowhere near freeing him.

Looking back, she watched as two Writhens circled Fenrir, and she fought the urge to run to his aid. She turned back to Forseti, and without preamble, slapped him across the face.

"Wake up," she yelled. "Tell me what to do."

She heard a scream and looked up to see Meruim being taken to the ground while Abba attempted to pull the beast off her.

Net held her ear to Forseti's chest, and thank all the gods, his heart was still beating. She began shaking him and yelling his name, anything to wake him, but again it was a lost cause. The entire mission was turning into a nightmare way worse than any she'd ever had.

The draw on her strength increased as if Hellion was speeding things along. Agomon could barely hold his sword up while Fenrir was gasping for air. After everything they'd been through and accomplished, it came down to this.

"I love you, Fenrir."

"I love you, my mate."

Their eyes met across the distance, both knowing they were nearing their final moments. Net's body slumped to the ground. Her ruby pendant slid off from her collarbone and landed on the ground. The small area around it turned to sand, causing her to remember where she'd found it initially and what occurred once she'd removed the pendant from the sand.

With what little strength she had left, Net clawed at the dry ground, making a small hole. She tore the pendant from the chain and shoved it down into the soil before covering it back up and laying her hand over it in a last-ditch attempt to protect it.

The ground began trembling again, or it might have been her.

Either way, she closed her eyes and waited for the end to come.

Chapter Fourteen

Net swatted at a fly, but the buzzing didn't stop as she'd hoped. Frustrated, she cracked her eyes open to get a look at the annoying bugger, but it was nowhere to be seen. The sun was shining in through the sheer drapes, and she wondered if she'd slept in because the sun was already high in the sky, and Fenrir was nowhere to be seen.

Raising her arms above her head, she stretched from the tips of her fingers to her toes before sitting up and grabbing her robe from the chair beside the bed. Tea sounded perfect, and she went in search of her delicious blend.

The worn floorboards felt warm against the soles of her feet as she walked to the kitchen, turned on the kettle, and pulled out her favorite mug. It felt good to be back at the cottage. She'd missed the peace and serenity of their home.

She'd begin her flower beds anew and add those strawberries she'd been considering. Then the buzzing started again. She waved her hands around her head but couldn't spy the offending fly anywhere in the air around her.

As her anger began to rise, Net realized she was no longer alone. She turned toward the living room to find Forseti sitting alone on the couch. He didn't look happy. What could she have done to anger him now?

"Forseti, to what do I owe this honor?" She'd stay as civil as possible until it was no longer an option.

His golden eyes turned in her direction before he said, "Net, come sit down. We need to talk."

"This can't be good," she replied as her mind raced with possible offenses. "Should we wait for Fenrir to return?"

He closed his eyes and took a deep breath. "He won't be returning here, Net."

Panic, sharp and ugly, raced through her system. "What do you mean? We live here. This is our home," she stated, dreading the answer while at the same time needing to know what was going on.

"Come sit down, and I will explain everything." Forseti kept motioning toward the chair positioned across from him as if that would make her move faster.

Something was wrong, very wrong. She felt it in her bones, but she did as Forseti asked and sat in the chair he'd directed her to. "Where is my mate?" Getting the most important question out of the way first was imperative for her to maintain her sanity.

Instead of answering, he asked her a question. "What is the last thing you remember?"

She was taken aback by the question. What was the last thing she remembered? "Easy, I…" Odd, before the buzzing, there was nothing. "Well, obviously, I went to bed and um…"

Forseti sat patiently, waiting as she concentrated harder, trying to sort through her memories. She and Fenrir had been together doing something, but she couldn't put her finger on what that something was. It was as if her memories had been erased.

"What's happened to my memories, and where is Fenrir?" She was becoming frantic. "Why can't I remember yesterday?"

"I will explain everything."

"Get to it," she ordered. The sooner this was figured out, the sooner she could get back to Fenrir.

Forseti let a small smile slip out of his usual stony façade. "You were always a pain in the ass. Do you remember anything about the mission you and Fenrir, as well as the four other gods, went on?"

"Mission?" The harder she thought about it, the more information began flooding her mind, as if a tap had been turned on full blast. "Hellion. Hellion, that evil nutjob, took you to a forest."

"Yes, the forest of souls," Forseti provided.

"He wants to be king." She remembered the fork-tongued bastard with grandiose dreams and an overinflated ego.

"Exactly. That was Hellion's plan. Once he'd drained me of my powers and assumed them as his own."

"There were Writhens and a tree that came to life. Meruim, Abba, Thiesen, and Agomon were with us in the forest. We had clues from Vruth, a Fae, and we went to that horrible place to free you." Memories began replaying like a movie in her mind.

"Yes, all of you did," Forseti confirmed.

"But the shield wouldn't hold and—" Net's mind began filling in the blanks like a crossword puzzle, and every scene led her to one conclusion. "I'm dead."

"Not yet." Had more foreboding words ever existed?

"What kind of answer is that?" she asked, looking for clarity before losing it altogether.

"An honest one."

"Is everyone else dead?" Her voice cracked with emotion at the thought. "Fenrir?"

"No, they are very much alive and well." Forseti seemed to brighten at being able to provide some good news.

Net could feel a weight being lifted off her chest, but she still had no idea what was going on. "You said I'm not dead yet. What does that mean exactly?" Was she fading away in the forest of souls? Couldn't be, Fenrir would have never left her behind.

"You entered the forest as a mortal, so Hellion drained more out of you than the others because you lacked the defenses to fight against it. Your immortality."

"So what you're saying is that I'm dying, but it hasn't happened yet."

"In a manner of speaking."

"I swear, Forseti, if you don't get to the point, I will slap you again," she threatened. She was tired of this back and forth and wanted the truth.

"Again?" Forseti asked.

"Never mind. Tell me what you've been avoiding saying." Now was not the time for games.

"Of all people, I would not have wished this decision to have to be made by you, but I have no other choice. Your mortal body is slipping away as we speak."

"So right now, we're in my mind while my real body is lying somewhere."

"Yes, in a medical clinic run by the Fae. They have done everything they can."

"What decision do I have to make?" Get to the point already if time was of the essence.

Forseti looked her straight in the eyes and said, "You have to decide on which form you will return in."

Net felt the blood draining from her face. "Sorry? Form?"

"Yes. Due to the damage done to your body and mind by the forest, your corporeal form is barely strong enough for one change. Either I return your powers to you, and you wake up as the Goddess Net once again, or I return you as mortal the same as you were without the chance of ever getting your powers back."

"Of course, I'd want the return of my powers, but I have a sick feeling there's a catch in there somewhere." Net knew better than to accept things at face value.

"You are correct. I did not want this for you, Net, but if I return your powers, your mating to Fenrir will be ended, and you will have no memory of him other than your friendship."

Net shook her head in disbelief. "It can't be. Haven't I paid enough?" She stood, unable to contain her anger. "First you blame me for your son's death, then you try to kill me, and finally, you overreached and maliciously took my powers. I risked my mortal life to save your godly ass, and this is how you repay me?"

Will this nightmare ever end?

"I receive no joy from any of this. That is why I'm leaving the choice up to you." True, he didn't look happy but had he ever? "I will be able to extend your life to sync with Fenrir's, which means if he dies for any reason, you will as well."

She walked over to the bay window and looked out to the beautiful forest beyond the cottage. "Does Fenrir know?"

"Yes."

"And what did he have to say about this?"

"Fenrir wanted me to give you your powers back. He would not deny you what you've wanted most."

"Wanted most?"

"Yes."

Net couldn't imagine putting Fenrir through the same pain she'd felt while watching her former mate be reborn without any knowledge of her or the love they had once shared. She couldn't imagine a life without Fenrir in it. What she wanted most was her mate.

"Send me back."

"In which form do you wish?"

"I'm stunned someone as all-powerful as yourself doesn't already know."

Profound sadness escaped his usual stoic persona before he had a chance to stop it. "When it comes to matters of the heart, I'm no authority."

Net began to see Forseti for the man he was and not the god. She'd not realized until this moment, he was dead inside. Emotion played no part in his decision-making.

***

Fenrir watched the rise and fall of his mate's chest. He'd have to remember not to call her by that endearment when she woke up. It would only confuse her because she'd have no memory of their mated life together. The irony wasn't lost on him. Fenrir had restored life to Net's former mate, but he was unable to transfer his memories. Now the same would happen to Net, and she wouldn't have memories of their mated life either. He now had a full appreciation of what Net had gone through.

Her alive and safe would have to warm him over the centuries to come. She'd remember him as they were before Forseti was taken, and that would be all he could hope to have. He took the opportunity to run his fingers through her golden hair one last time and couldn't stop the tears from forming in the corner of his eyes.

Net had fought hard to do everything that was expected from her. She'd freed Forseti by figuring out the ruby's sole purpose. In hindsight, it all made sense. They had to destroy the forest to free Forseti, and the stone did that as it had done among rock towers that turned out to be islands.

The forest of souls held no power now, and those who had still been trapped there were freed. Hellion and his group had disappeared and were still being hunted. The Writhens scattered along with the remaining ogres and demons.

Without Fenrir's courageous mate, none of this would have been possible. The worlds would be forced to live in fear of those who, on a whim, wished to exert their power over them. Net deserved to receive her powers back. She needed to be able to be the realms' Divine Mother, and she needed to be able to protect herself.

Somehow, Fenrir would learn how to live over again.

Net's fingers began to flex as Forseti appeared in the room. "She has made her choice."

"Thank you for saving her."

"I owe Net much more than can ever be properly repaid, but I will endeavor to do so." With a nod, Forseti was gone.

"Fenrir?" Net's raspy voice had him turning.

He looked down into those beautiful jade green eyes, steeling himself for the worst. "Yes, Net, I am here. You are safe, and it's going to stay that way."

"Of course, I'm going to be safe." Net smiled wide. "I'll be with my mate."

Fenrir blinked a few times before saying, "I'm sorry. Can you say that again?'

Net sat up on the bed and cupped the side of his face. "I said, I'll be safe with my mate. You."

Fenrir realized that he couldn't feel any powers coming from her. She hadn't returned a goddess. She had chosen to remain his mate.

He rose from his chair and lifted her into his arms, holding her tight to his chest. "You chose me over your powers?"

"Of course. It was easy, really. I can live without my powers, but I cannot live without you."

Fenrir had never heard sweeter words spoken. He relayed what Net had chosen to their other team members and teleported them back home to their cottage. They stood in the center of their living room back in the place where this crazy journey all began.

The painting, blankets, and throw pillows were all where they'd left them when he'd reconstructed the cottage in another realm.

Fenrir could finally breathe again as he looked down at his beloved mate. He pulled her close and said, "Welcome home, mate."

"Our home." Net sighed. "I'm so happy to be back here. Are we in our original forest?"

"Yes, and there should be no need to leave it again until we want to." Fenrir had fought to guarantee that, even though the fact that Vengier was still out there somewhere lingered like a foul taste on Fenrir's tongue.

"Oh, and look," Net said, waved her arm, producing the same whip she'd created using Forseti's shield. "Pretty cool."

"He gave you a new shield?" Fenrir asked, hoping it was true. Net returned as a mortal, and she needed some sort of protection, considering the traitors were still on the loose.

"I guess. I felt it when I woke up, but I was so happy to see you, I forgot it was there."

"This gift is so welcome. You have no idea what it does to my heart, knowing you will be protected when I'm not near you."

"Well, I plan on being by your side for many centuries to come, considering Forseti also synced up our lives. Allowing me to live as long as you do."

Apparently, Forseti had done all he could to make this transition as painless as possible, but Fenrir still had to know.

"Are you sure this is what you want? I know you were looking forward to getting your powers back and were having a difficult time with the fragility of a mortal body." Fenrir had to confirm that his mate was happy with her choice. Net had already given up so much over the centuries, and he didn't want her to regret her decision.

Net wrapped her arms around his neck and smiled. "Here, in our home and in your arms, is the only place I want to be. You are my home, Fenrir, the home I'd been missing for longer than I care to think about. I finally have everything I've ever wanted. You."

Fenrir lowered his lips to his mate's and poured his love through their connection.

The years wouldn't always be easy for them, but Fenrir was positive that with Net by his side, it would always be exciting and filled with love.

Chapter Fifteen

Meruim waited for the others to arrive. This whole being summoned thing rubbed her the wrong way. However, there wasn't much that could be done about it, so she leaned back against the patio chair and took in the warm sunlight shining down upon her. The sky was blue, and the birds were singing. It'd become so pleasant she almost forgot where she was.

"I see you've made yourself at home already." Abba's voice didn't even make her jump. She'd felt him arrive.

"If I have to wait, then why not do it comfortably?" she asked while raising her hands and placing them behind her head.

"I'll give you that one." Abba chuckled before taking a look around.

"Did I hear someone speaking about comfort?" Thiesen asked with a hopeful expression as he joined their little group.

Agomon waved out his arm. "Meruim, lounging around again," he said, grinning.

She let out a huff and slowly sat up. "Now that the gang's all here, what the hell do you guys want?" The other three turned to one another, looking confused and unsure, giving her pause.

"I didn't plan this reunion. It seems Fenrir and Net haven't arrived yet," Abba answered.

"That's because they are not coming," Forseti's voice rang out, making Meruim groan.

"What have we done wrong now?" she asked, not bothering to wait for the browbeating to begin.

"Why does everyone always assume that?" Forseti grumbled. "I cannot help that I'm The Judge, but there is more to me."

"Okay, then where are Fenrir and Net?" Thiesen asked, and Meruim was wondering the same thing. She hadn't seen either of them in several months.

"Awaiting the arrival of their first child, a daughter." For a brief moment, The Judge looked happy, but it was gone so fast that Meruim questioned if she ever indeed saw it at all.

"Good for them," Abba announced. "It's about time those two got the happiness they deserve.

Meruim would have to remember to pop in on them after the birth to meet the new arrival. "Okay, so why are we here?"

"Many reasons, not the least of which is your ability to work together. Gods typically don't do well with being a team as most feel the need to lead. However, your group managed to combine your powers to search out the clues and fight as one."

"Well, the years I've spent in training—" Whatever Agomon was about to say was cut short.

"Blah, blah, blah, I'm the warrior god, blah, blah, blah." Meruim groaned. "Buttering us up before you lay down the gavel isn't going to work, Forseti. What do you want?"

"Straight to the point, I respect that," Forseti stated. "I want the four of you to join the hunt for the traitors responsible for the death and destruction of the innocent beings living in all the different realms while I was held prisoner, including the gods who joined Hellion. Those who chose to join the side of evil and harmed innocents must be judged."

"Let me get this straight," Abba said. "You want us to become your bounty hunters?"

"If that is a term you prefer, then yes, bounty hunters," Forseti agreed.

"I'm sorry, but that term suggests payment for services," Meruim stated. "Is that what you're saying?"

"Leave it to you to think of your own gain when it's our duty to find these traitors and bring them to justice," Agomon preached.

"Calm yourself, oh great warrior. Some of us may not be so willing to risk our lives so easily. All I'm saying is that there has to be something to compensate us for the time, frustration, and pain coming our way if we agree to this."

"Always the shrewd one," Abba said, and she wasn't sure if he meant that as a compliment or a shit-shot.

"Someone has to be." She went with a shit-shot.

"I agree that there should be some sort of remuneration for your time and troubles." Forseti didn't look put out by her request, making her wonder how dangerous a mission they were about to undertake.

"Now we're talking." Meruim leaned back in her chair once again, striking a relaxed pose.

"What do you have in mind?" Thiesen asked as he took a seat beside Meruim.

"I will strike a bargain with each of you. For every traitor you bring to me to be judged, your team will receive a single *desire*. The standard caveats for said *desire* are the causing of no harm to another being, force another being to do something against their will, or to increase one's own power. The *desire* benefits the recipients without harming another."

Now that was an offer that got her attention. Being given an opportunity like this didn't come around very often. Forseti was the one god that held the power needed to make what she desperately wanted to happen.

"I'm in," she announced.

"Wow, that was quick." Abba chuckled. "You sure you don't want to think about it?"

"No need, I accept the terms."

"You have my bond, Meruim," Forseti confirmed that they had struck an accord.

"Wait, you said the team gets one *desire*." Thiesen pointed out. "But there are four of us."

"You are correct," Forseti responded. "The four of you must agree on a single *desire* each time you bring me a traitor."

"Damn." Meruim should have looked at the fine print before agreeing. "We can take turns then."

"How do we decide who gets the first opportunity?" Agomon asked, suddenly interested in their discussion. Meruim couldn't help but wonder what it was he secretly wanted.

"You're going to allow us to have whatever we wish for?" Abba asked, sounding a bit skeptical.

"As long as no one is harmed, free will is maintained, and there is no increase to your personal powers, yes."

"Aren't you afraid that we'll misuse what you give us?' Abba asked. Why did the god always come up with the ethical side of things?

"That is why it takes all four of you to agree on one choice," Forseti explained.

"So, between the four of us, you're hoping there's enough ethical and logical reasoning to stop one of us from taking advantage of this opportunity," Thiesen summarized.

"That is exactly what I'm counting on. If there is something you desire most of all, then each of you will have to convince the others to agree."

What did she have to lose? "I'm still in." She'd figure out a way to bring the other three around to her way of thinking.

"Okay, I'm in as well," Abba stated but didn't look overly happy about it.

"Me too," Thiesen agreed.

"I still believe we should consider this an honor, not a bargaining chip," Agomon protested.

"Fine. We'll skip you when it's your turn to choose," Thiesen suggested. "You are more than welcome to do as you've said and accept only the honor of a job well done. As for me, I'll take the fulfilling of a *desire*."

Agomon huffed out a frustrated breath. "I'll do it if only to keep the three of you from making horrible decisions."

"I accept the four of your statements as your vow. A contract has been struck," Forseti announced without preamble.

"Now, let's begin."

ABOUT THE AUTHOR

Lilli Carlisle lives in the country near Toronto, Canada. She is the mother of two wonderful girls, wife to an amazing man, and servant to the pets in her life, and she's a member of Toronto Romance Writers. Lilli writes paranormal romance, and believes love should be celebrated and shared. After all, everybody needs a little romance, excitement, intrigue, and passion in their lives.

Connect with Lilli:

Instagram:/lillicarlisle

facebook.com/lillicarlisleauthor

twitter.com/LilliCarlisle

www.BOROUGHSPUBLISHINGGROUP.com

If you enjoyed this book, please write a review. Our authors appreciate the feedback, and it helps future readers find books they love. We welcome your comments and invite you to send them to info@boroughspublishinggroup.com. Follow us on Facebook, Twitter and Instagram, and be sure to sign up for our newsletter for surprises and new releases from your favorite authors.

Are you an aspiring writer? Check out www.boroughspublishinggroup.com/submit and see if we can help you make your dreams come true.

www.ingramcontent.com/pod-product-compliance
Lightning Source LLC
Chambersburg PA
CBHW030316130626
46549CB00002B/889